Wild in Love

~ The Maverick Billionaires ~

Book 5

Bella Andre & Jennifer Skully

WILD IN LOVE

~ The Maverick Billionaires, Book 5 ~

Meet the Maverick Billionaires—sexy, self-made men from the wrong side of town who survived hell together and now have everything they ever wanted. But when each Maverick falls head over heels for an incredible woman he never saw coming, he will soon find that true love is the only thing he ever really needed...

Daniel Spencer is proud of the billion-dollar business he's built, but there are few things he enjoys more than creating something with his bare hands. Lake Tahoe has everything he's looking for—the cabin he's building for family and friends to enjoy, crystal clear water, and lush green mountains. Everything except the perfect woman to share it with. Until Tasha Summerfield literally falls into his arms.

After learning that her family has lied to her for pretty much her entire life, Tasha flees San Francisco for the mountains. As she tries to bury her heartache by hammering her dilapidated cabin back together, the last thing she expects is to fall for a sexy billionaire. But when a storm blows in and she desperately needs help, there is Daniel, waiting with open arms.

Tasha believes Daniel deserves a woman from a perfect, loving, tight-knit family like his. Yet how can she possibly resist a man this sweet and generous…who looks positively sinful in his tool belt? With every delicious taste of him, Tasha finds it harder to quell the hopes and dreams she thought were crushed forever. But when it turns out that Daniel's family isn't picture perfect after all, will the truth set them both free? Or will it destroy any chance they ever had?

A note from Bella & Jennifer

As soon as we started writing about the Maverick Billionaires, emails flooded our inboxes, all wanting to know the same thing—when was Daniel going to get his happily-ever-after?

At long last, we are thrilled to give you the story you've been waiting for. We absolutely loved writing Daniel and Tasha's story. And we loved the setting too. Lake Tahoe is a beautiful part of California that we love to visit.

Thank you for supporting our Mavericks—and our writing dreams. We hope you absolutely adore *Wild In Love*!

Happy reading,
Bella and Jennifer

P.S. More Mavericks are coming soon! Please sign up for our New Release newsletters for more information. BellaAndre.com/Newsletter and bit.ly/SkullyNews

Chapter One

The lake was brilliantly blue and perfectly calm as Daniel Spencer stood on the back deck of his Tahoe getaway. The air held the crisp scent of the mountains, and he breathed deeply to take in the sweetness. He'd chosen Fallen Leaf Lake on which to build his waterfront cabin because of this spectacular view, the snow-capped mountains in the distance, the scent of wildflowers just starting to bloom, and the peace of it all, away from the rush and noise of the city.

Except for the insistent *thwack* of a staple gun spoiling the perfect quiet.

Since his last visit over three months ago, someone must have moved into the run-down shack up the hill—the blue tarps on the roof were new, and a small, older-model truck had replaced the rusted hulk on the gravel drive. He'd always gotten along well with his neighbors, but this morning he couldn't push away his resentment at the intrusion.

His family had been right; he definitely needed a few days away to recharge. It had been way too long since he'd had a vacation, or come up to work on the cabin. Weekends had been out of the question as well, given that they had become a revolving door of birthday parties and sports events and barbecues with his friends and their wives or girlfriends and children.

The other four Mavericks—Will, Sebastian, Matt, and Evan—had each found the woman of their dreams. A partner they could share everything with. Love and companionship and intimacy. Over the past few months, Daniel had begun to realize that being the only unattached Maverick separated him from the pack.

He was now the odd man out.

Will's wedding had jump-started Daniel's restlessness—and Evan and Paige's recent housewarming party had only deepened the growing hole inside him. At first, he'd sought to plug it with work, making sure he had little time for anything else—especially thinking too much. But he had to admit he'd become a bear to work for these past few months, asking for too much, pushing everyone else as hard as he pushed himself.

And all the while, he couldn't help asking himself, what was it all for? He'd triumphed over his dirt-poor childhood to build Top Notch DIY into the world's leading home-improvement franchise, with outlets around the globe. His face filled millions of screens on a homebuilding TV show that aired weekly. He had more money than he could possibly spend. But something was missing.

Some*one* was missing.

Someone to share it all with.

At thirty-six, Daniel had dated plenty of women, but he'd never found the one woman with whom he could share the perfect love and relationship he'd seen in his parents. It had never felt sappy to say that he wanted the kind of love his mom and dad had found. After all, who wouldn't want a relationship that good, that free of bumps and hurdles—two people who had always been there for each other, no matter what?

His mother, Susan Spencer, set the bar. As an adult, Daniel had a clear-eyed view of her strength and wisdom, qualities he hadn't always appreciated as a punk kid narrowly skirting the line between right and wrong. Back then, he hadn't wanted his father's no-nonsense advice either. But Daniel knew better now. His parents were his rocks, his guides. They never faltered, never screwed up, even though they had struggled to make ends meet for most of their lives.

No matter how difficult life had been, they'd never lost sight of the important things: love, family, loyalty. In that grimy Chicago neighborhood, which was the only place they could afford, Bob and Susan Spencer had taken in his friends—all the Mavericks—and though each of the boys had gone through his own struggles, none of them had ever been left wanting for love or attention.

Daniel had been thinking of his family when he'd drawn the plans for this cabin. It wasn't meant to be a bachelor pad—he envisioned playing games outside in the summer sun with his wife and kids and making s'mores in the outdoor fire pit beneath a full moon.

At present, the exterior was complete except for the trimmings. He had electricity as well as plumbing, one working bathroom, and a carefully handcrafted river-rock fireplace. The refrigerator, countertop microwave and coffee machine were the only working appliances in the kitchen, but he did all the real cooking on the barbecue anyway. He'd brought in a big bed for his master suite so he had somewhere decent to sleep, but though the log walls were dried in, there were holes where the interior door frames should be and bare, unfinished planks for floors. For all his dreams, the house wasn't much more than a shell.

Just like his life.

He shook his head, cursing himself for falling into a mental hole again. This week away from work was supposed to renew him. He'd risen hours before dawn in order to miss the commuter traffic on the drive up from San Francisco. On the road, he'd been eager to continue the work. Now that he was here, it was time to focus on the fact that he was not only the luckiest guy in the world to have a thriving business and bank account, along with all his close friends, but also that nothing he'd faced would ever compare to his parents' struggles. Especially not while he was standing on the edge of a glorious blue lake, with the Memorial Day holiday just around the corner and a week's vacation stretching out ahead of him.

He knew exactly what would knock some sense back into his brain—a cannonball into the frigid lake. The ice and snow that had covered the water for the past several months had only just melted.

He whipped off his flannel shirt, kicked off his boots and jeans, and had just made a flying leap toward the crystal clear water when a scream suddenly fractured the morning's quiet.

* * *

Tasha Summerfield had never actually believed one's entire life could flash before them in the moment they were about to die.

She believed it now.

Five minutes ago, with her tools dangling from the belt around her hips, she'd been climbing carefully up onto the roof. The weatherman predicted a thunderstorm would roll in by Friday, and the tarp she'd tacked up to cover all the leaks had torn loose.

Her roofline was steeply sloped, which thankfully meant the snow from the previous week's storm was already sliding off rather than piling high. Unfortunately, it also made it tough to position herself properly to tack down the squares of plastic tarp with a staple gun.

Holding the edge, she'd gotten her hand too close to the staple gun and almost nailed her thumb.

"Watch what you're doing, Tasha."

She'd become way too used to talking to herself over the past three months, but it was either talk to herself like a crazy lady, or go absolutely nuts from the unending silence.

Besides, anything was better than thinking about her family.

Having forcefully shaken thoughts of her father and brother from her head, she'd just finished nailing down the last corner of the tarp when the extra box of staples in its pouch in her tool belt tumbled out, broke open, and scattered.

Grabbing for them, she'd not only missed, she'd also gone tumbling down the roof, scrabbling for a handhold, but finding none.

And as all twenty-seven years of her life flashed by, one particularly horrible scene stood out in vivid Technicolor.

Chapter Two

Three months ago…

The view from her father's office window was magnificent, the San Francisco Bay darkly powerful as a storm rolled in from the north. Tasha's brother, Drew, stood by the window, his arms folded over his chest, his face a tense mask as dark as the leaden sky behind him. Five years older than Tasha, Drew had the same black hair they'd inherited from their mother, his cut scrupulously short, executive style, like their father's.

Seated in front of her father's dominating oak desk was Eric Whitcomb III, a partner in Lakeside Ventures with her father and Drew. Tasha had been dating Eric for almost a year. He'd bowled her over the day her dad had introduced him—at thirty-nine, he was charming, handsome, and cultured. She felt like a character on *Downton Abbey* when she was with him. Wined and dined and desired by an English gentleman.

"Sit down, Natasha," Reggie Summerfield ordered.

He was a loving father, but he was also a man who instantly commanded respect, so she put down her bag and sat on the sofa facing him. Even seated behind his massive desk, her father was an imposing man, with steel-gray hair and eyes so dark they were almost black.

She felt spotlighted in his gaze, the look in his eyes reminding her of all the times as a child that he had called her into his home office—wherever home had been at the time—and told her they had to move again. At least once a year, sometimes more, she'd had to leave her friends, her school, the teachers she loved, whatever clubs she'd joined. *Poof*—no warning, just gone. She'd lost count of the times she'd started over in a new place.

Her stomach was already clenched with that familiar anxiety as she asked, "Is something wrong?" She wasn't a kid anymore, so it wasn't her childhood fears of making new friends that held her in their grip this time. Instead, they were the worries of a daughter with an aging parent, one who meant the world to her. Was her father sick? Was that why Drew and Eric were both here? Could that be the reason her brother looked so grave and sad?

"We're canceling the venture," her father said. "You need to lie low for a while." He hiked his tailor-made slacks and crossed his legs. For a man who never fidgeted, she could swear that was exactly what he was doing. "Take a trip like you've always wanted to do."

Relief washed through her that he hadn't sprung an illness on her. But what on earth was he talking about? "You're shutting down Lakeside Ventures? Why would you do that?"

"We need to take down the website too," he replied in lieu of answering her questions. He twirled a pen on his desk, another uncharacteristic movement. "And it would be best if you shut down your business as well." He punctuated the words with an ominous drumming of his fingers on the chair arms.

"Shut down my *business*?" It was unthinkable— what would she tell her clients? She designed interactive websites as well as marketing collateral and had recently entered the field of interactive commercials. A year ago, her father had hired her to do the website for Lakeside Ventures. The enterprise was going to revolutionize timeshares, and she'd been so happy to be a part of it, because everything her father touched turned to gold. But now he wanted her to erase everything she'd worked for since she'd graduated from college five years ago? "Why would I do that? The website is good." Really good, if she did say so herself.

"The website is fantastic, Tasha." It was the first thing Drew had said, jumping to her defense. Drew leveled his piercing blue gaze on their father. "Tell her the truth, Dad."

Seated across from her father, Eric snorted, shaking his head, looking anywhere but at her. He seemed a different man from the one who'd meticulously planned tomorrow night's Valentine's dinner, telling her he would be sending a limo to pick her up, promising her a present that would thrill her. She'd been imagining a small velvet box...and had secretly wondered if she was truly ready for everything Eric might offer.

Her father's next words dashed all her contemplations. "We're under investigation."

He couldn't have stunned her more if he'd dangled her outside the twentieth-floor window by her heels. "Investigation? By whom?" Nothing made sense, not from the moment she'd walked in and found the atmosphere inside her father's office as dark and stormy as the view outside.

"The government. They say it's fraud. We just haven't gotten our funding yet, and a few antsy clients are questioning what we're doing."

The first Lakeside resort—to be followed by many more—was in Northern California. Tasha had wanted to visit the building site before now, but her brother had convinced her she was too busy working on the state-of-the-art website—and keeping up with her other client projects—to take time off just yet. Using the photos of the lake and surrounding woods that Drew and her father had supplied, along with the architects' plans, she'd graphically created what the resort would look like, down to the interiors of the individual condos.

It was impossible that the government could question her father or her brother. It had to be a terrible error.

She would do everything in her power to stop this

miscarriage of justice. Her father couldn't give up everything he'd worked so hard for. And they definitely couldn't do this to Drew. He'd been so proud when their dad asked him to join the family business after he'd graduated from high school—she still remembered their celebration.

"We can fix this, Dad," she said, jumping off the couch, passion filling her to right this wrong. "We'll give the investigators the plans. I'll walk them through the website, show them how great it's going to be once you've got all the funding. And when you take them up to the site where the condos are going to be built, you'll be exonerated, and we can get back to building the resort."

"Grow up, Tasha." Eric's harsh voice sliced through her pleas, cutting them to ribbons. "It's time you faced a few facts."

Over the past five minutes, more than one surprise had been tossed Tasha's way. But the biggest one of all was the change in the man she'd been dating. Gone was the smooth, British accent, the cultured Eric-Whitcomb-the-Third façade now replaced by a flat American tone. Gone were the handsome features, erased by a hard mouth curled in an ugly sneer. "Your dad wants you to lie low, so just do what he says and get the hell out of town until this blows over."

She stared at him, stunned. Eric had seemed so perfect, always so nice, so solicitous. But she remembered that he'd only once told her the name of his family's so-called estate. And hadn't they always gone out with her friends, rather than any of his?

It all made sense now. He wasn't who he'd said he was. And he'd obviously duped her father and brother into some sort of disreputable scheme.

She came at him, ready to pounce, desperate to avenge her family. "What have you suckered my family into?"

Eric laughed, a cruel, grating sound. Which wouldn't have stopped her from coming after him, had he not followed it up with, "Honey, your father brought *me* into the deal. We've worked a couple of cons together before—I've always been brilliant at playing the charming front man." He smiled wide, like a shark, once more affecting his cultured British accent. "Downright convincing, if I do say so myself."

Her brother cut across the animosity brimming between the two of them. "Shut up, Eric."

Eric snarled like an angry jungle cat. "Then tell her she'd better get the hell out of Dodge before we're all arrested. I don't want her talking to anyone."

"Leave." Her father's voice snapped Eric's words in half. "Now."

"Fine. I'll go. Just take care of this little—"

She'd never know what contemptuous name Eric was going to call her, because Drew was suddenly there, his hand around Eric's biceps, dragging him from the chair. He tossed Eric out of the office, slamming the door behind him.

Tasha waited for her father to deny everything. She waited for Drew to do the same.

But there were no denials.

Instead, all her father said was, "It would be better if you disappeared for a while."

Disappeared. As though she'd done something wrong.

Oh God. All those times they'd moved…

Was this the reason?

"Is it really true?" She couldn't make her voice rise above a whisper. Couldn't stop her limbs from shaking. "Was the resort just a big scam?"

Her father started to get up from his chair. "Sweetheart—"

She cringed. Then she looked at Drew, who still stood immobile by the door.

"I'm sorry, Tash."

Turning on her father, she lashed out. "You used my website to *con people*?"

The higher her voice rose, the lower her father's fell. "On the books, you were just a contractor. You'll be fine, sweetheart."

She wanted to scream at him never to use that endearment again.

Drew reached for her hand, but stopped himself before he actually touched her. "That's why we never wanted you to go to the building site. So no one could point a finger at you. And I made sure that you could never track—" He stopped, shut down by the look their father flashed him.

But she could barely hear what he was saying as her brain went round and round with what she'd just learned. Was this why her father had encouraged her college degree in web design and development? He must have seen the potential of her skills to bilk money out of unsuspecting victims and had just been biding his time until the perfect opportunity came along.

The perfect con.

It was *monstrous*.

"I'm so sorry, Tash," her brother said again in an anguished voice. "I never meant to let you get hurt."

But he'd been a part of it all. They'd both lied to her. Used her. She needed to think straight, needed to figure out how long this had been going on. "What did Eric mean, that he knew you and Dad from other cons?"

Her father spoke before Drew could. "We've worked with Eric before, that's all. No big deal."

She couldn't believe he was trying to blow her off like she didn't have ears to hear with or a head to think with. But maybe, it suddenly occurred to her, she didn't. Otherwise, wouldn't she have spotted the lies? Lies that must have started way back, when she was just a little girl? Before that, even.

"He used the word *con*," she said, her voice getting stronger now. Harder. "Not *job*. And he said I could be arrested."

In typical evasive fashion, her father said, "No one's

going to arrest you. We've already explained that."

Growing up, she'd never questioned how her father paid for their fancy apartments and luxury cars, or the five-star vacations and her private school. All she'd known was that he was in "investments" like so many of her girlfriends' fathers. She'd never let herself wonder too hard about why they'd so frequently had to pack up at a moment's notice, always leaving so much behind.

But now, with the blindfold ripped from her eyes, she realized that in every single instance, her father must have been running away from whatever shady deal he'd had going.

How could she have been so blind?

"Are you a con man?" She needed to hear him say it.

He waved his hands. "That's such a misnomer."

Before she could reply to that ridiculous statement, Drew added, "We liberate money from people who are too stupid to make good use of it."

She turned her head just enough to stare at her brother. He sounded like a parrot, repeating a phrase someone had taught him. A phrase *their father* had taught him.

"We never go after old people or the vulnerable," Drew continued in what she was sure he thought must be a reasonable tone. "Only people who don't deserve the kind of money they have. People who inherited a big chunk of money they didn't work for, or cash they came by nefariously."

This couldn't be her brother, whom she'd loved and looked up to since she was a kid. Drew's biggest goal in life had been to join their father's company and make their dad proud of him. But he'd clearly been brainwashed by the great Reggie Summerfield into thinking that stealing was okay as long as you stole from people who didn't "deserve" the money.

All so that her father could turn his son into a criminal.

Anger roiled, bubbling up to overwhelm her as she rounded on her father. "I can't believe you did this to Drew. I can't believe you gave me a commission to make a website so that you could bamboozle unsuspecting people into giving you money for nothing." Perhaps that should have been the worst of it, but it was his more personal crimes against her that made the bile rise higher in her throat. "And that you would do something so disgusting as encouraging me to date your partner in crime!"

She was about to be sick all over the expensive hardwood floors...paid for with stolen money.

"Sweetheart. It's not as bad as you think." Her father's tone was conciliatory, cajoling, as though he could bring her around with pretty words.

"I *trusted* you." Because they were family, and family was never supposed to hurt you.

How could she ever trust anyone again when she couldn't even believe in her own flesh and blood? The worst was losing Drew. That was so much harder than losing Eric. No wonder she hadn't known how she'd react to the idea of a little velvet box and a marriage proposal. Somewhere down deep, she must have known her boyfriend couldn't possibly be for real.

But she'd never suspected her own father and brother weren't for real either.

"There's no way anything can come back on you," her father said. Still no apologies. No remorse. "But it would be better for you to get out of town before the investigators come to question you."

That was all Tasha could take. She couldn't bear to listen to one more excuse or horrible truth.

With one last look at her brother—and not one glance to spare for her father—Tasha ran.

* * *

She kept on running until she found seclusion in the mountains of South Lake Tahoe, then bought the run-down cabin super cheap, hoping the work to fix it up would occupy her mind to the exclusion of everything else.

During the last three months, she'd installed a shower, toilet, and bathroom sink. She had electricity, running water, and mounted a wood-burning stove so she wouldn't freeze. She would have turned off the Internet to further isolate herself from the rest of the world, but when her fixer-upper needed way more work than she'd anticipated, she needed her computer to watch how-to videos on carpentry, plumbing, electrical, and cement work. But apart from watching DIY videos, she'd scrubbed her existence from email, Facebook, and all other social media, and spent no additional time online.

Since leaving San Francisco, she'd returned to the city only once for a handful of days to meet with the investigators. She'd not only given back her commission for building the Lakeside Ventures website—she would never keep ill-gotten gains—she'd also told the investigators what she knew about the resort scam, which wasn't much, given that she had no idea where her father or brother had gone; they'd disappeared like wisps of fog in the sun. Thankfully, the authorities had managed to freeze the business accounts, with most of the money intact, so that the bulk of the bilked investors would receive reparations.

In the end, the investigators had let her go, believing she hadn't known the true nature of the resort con. In her heart, though, she still felt corrupted, not only by this scam, but by all the times she hadn't asked questions about the other ones.

During her final days in the city, she'd finished up the last of her website contracts, then shut down her business. She missed brainstorming with her clients, helping them bring their visions to life, building something that could potentially change their lives for the better. After losing her father, her brother, and her boyfriend, throwing her business into the gutter had damn near broken the last piece of her heart. But she couldn't allow herself to keep any lifeline to the real world.

Especially when it hadn't been real at all.

These past months, she'd desperately missed conversation, missed shooting the breeze with someone, anyone. Apart from *hello* and *how are you* with the clerks at the grocery and hardware stores, she hadn't had a meaningful conversation with a single person since she'd come to Tahoe. She hadn't called any of her friends before she went underground, simply sent a group email to say she'd been overworking and needed a break so she'd be gone awhile—like *forever*. Then she'd ditched her phone so she wouldn't be tempted to call anyone.

She missed her friends terribly. But if she reached out to any of them, how could she ever tell them what an idiot she'd been? And, far worse, how could she ever atone for the lives that had been ruined because she hadn't woken up earlier to the con that was her life?

Loneliness was what she deserved. Loneliness was her punishment.

All she had was this cabin. This was her home now, the only home she could truly say was *hers* after how rootless her father's existence had kept them all. She had the clean air and the cool lake. In time, she might deserve more, but for now, she'd exiled herself to this little corner of the world until she could learn how to judge people's motives correctly. Until she could remember never to take anything at face value. Until she could figure out what was so wrong with her that she made excuses for people rather than face the truth.

She'd thought she had such a great life, a fabulous boyfriend, a loving family. But it had all been a sham. Even the good memories couldn't be trusted. They were just illusions. Only this lake, this cabin, this clean crisp air, and the birds chattering loudly in the trees above were real.

As real as the terror shooting through her as she tumbled toward the edge of the roof—and a fall that was certain to do as much damage to her body as her family had done to her heart.

Chapter Three

Daniel surfaced as quickly as he could, then scrambled to get out of the water and into his jeans and boots. Still dripping wet and shirtless, he took the hill like an Olympic sprinter, his lungs bursting. He couldn't slow down, not after the terror he'd heard in that scream. One horrible scenario after another ran through his head. A hiker lying at the bottom of a ravine with two broken legs. Swarmed by yellow jackets. Or worse.

He rounded the corner of the derelict cabin, and his heart lunged into his throat at the sight of the figure dangling from the rooftop, clinging to the bent gutter by her fingers. Which were starting to slip.

"Don't let go," he yelled. "I'm getting the ladder." Thankfully, it was only a dozen feet away, and he quickly dragged it over. "Reach out with your leg and you'll be able to put your foot on it."

When she didn't move, he realized the woman must be too dazed by fear to follow his instructions. Climbing the rungs, he grabbed her around the waist and pulled her against him.

"I've got you." He instinctively hugged her tighter,

as though to reassure himself she wasn't in danger of falling again. "You can let go of the gutter now."

The metal was so rusted it would have torn off in another second. She was damned lucky it hadn't ripped away with the impact of her fall.

The vision of what might have happened was so bloody that he had to work to gentle his voice. "Go ahead and put your hands on the ladder."

But she still clung tenaciously to the metal gutter, her knuckles white.

"It's okay," he murmured in a low, soothing voice against the dark hair trailing out of her ball cap, the bright sun glossing her long braid blue-black. She seemed so small, draped in the folds of her overalls. "I won't let you fall."

Finally, her knuckle-breaking grip eased, and on a shaky exhale, she put one hand on the ladder, followed by the other.

"I've got you," he said again as he bracketed her on the ladder. "Tell me when you think you're ready to make it all the way down."

She didn't answer for a long moment, finally saying, "I'm ready."

Her voice was soft, musical, playing an accompaniment to the pounding of his heart and the rushing in his blood.

Easing down a rung, then another, he kept his hand on her waist as they made their way together. Back on the ground, he had to force himself to let her go.

He'd never had this kind of instant reaction to a woman before. Then again, he'd never rescued a woman hanging off the edge of a roof either. There was certainly something to be said for a massive adrenaline rush.

Standing before him, she wasn't nearly as small as she'd seemed up on the ladder, only a few inches shorter than he was. The voluminous overalls and tool belt had made her seem tiny in comparison. She was in her mid-twenties, he guessed, with high cheekbones, long lashes, blue-as-the-sky eyes, and a luscious form his mother would have smacked him for looking at the way he couldn't help looking. Especially given that he had no business drooling when she was clearly still in shock.

She held on to a rung of the ladder to steady herself, her eyes scrunched closed as she said, "I don't know what happened. One minute I was on the roof nailing down the tarp—and the next I was clinging to the gutter for dear life." She opened her eyes and looked up at the roof. "I guess it isn't *that* big a drop, and I might have been okay if I'd fallen, but it all happened so fast, I couldn't think straight."

She turned to him then, and both her eyes and her mouth opened wide as she looked from his bare chest, to his wet jeans, then deliberately down to a big rock sticking up out of the ground ten feet away.

He'd completely forgotten he was shirtless—or that his jeans were sticking to his thighs like a second skin.

All that had mattered was getting to her as quickly as possible.

"I'm standing here babbling," she said in a voice that suddenly sounded a little breathless, "when what I should be saying is thank you."

There were a good half-dozen nice things he could have said to get her over the shock of falling from the roof—starting with *You're welcome*—but as the full impact of what might have happened slammed into him, he was blinded to anything but the danger in which she'd so foolishly put herself.

"You might have broken a leg." His voice was harsh from the realization that he could just as easily have found her on the ground. "Or worse, depending on how you fell. First of all, you shouldn't have gone up on the roof alone. And second, you should have secured yourself. Your roof has a helluva steep incline. Why didn't you wait for someone—if not someone you hired, then friends or family—to help you do the work?"

He thought he saw sorrow darken her ocean-blue eyes for a split second before she threw her shoulders back and said, "I've been doing a pretty darn good job of fixing up this place without anyone to help me." Her expression turned rueful as she admitted, "Until today, at least."

He forced himself to drag his gaze away from her to eye the cabin. "I thought they were going to tear this place down." The wood siding was sun-bleached, the window frames cracked, and the front porch, visible around the corner of the house, sagged like an old couch. On closer inspection, though, he saw she'd replaced the rotted boards by the front door.

He couldn't believe anyone would buy this place. He didn't know if he admired her for it...or just plain thought she was nuts.

As though she could read his mind, she put her hands on her hips and said, "I can fix it."

"Right." He meant it noncommittally, just a word to say to a beautiful woman who was making odd things happen inside his chest.

But she took it as a challenge. "I'm still working on the roof, obviously. But I've done a lot inside. Here, I'll show you." She marched up the porch steps, assuming he would follow.

Naturally, he did, enjoying her vivid defiance—and her surprisingly luscious curves—more than he'd enjoyed anything in a very long time. Even if he was still upset with her for getting up on the roof without a safety line.

But before he could get all twisted up about that again, he suddenly noticed the words stitched on her ball cap. "Do I need to worry?" He pointed to the top of her head.

She ran her fingertips over the lettering, saying aloud what was printed across the cap: "*Zombie Apocalypse First Responder.*" She shrugged as though it was a perfectly normal hat to be wearing. "Trust me, you'll be happy for my training if a zombie ever comes this way."

She didn't see the smile he couldn't control as she turned.

Hell yes, he'd follow. His mother would have used the word *smitten*. But really, the woman was too damn cute not to capture the attention of any red-blooded male within smiting distance.

Then again, what kind of woman bought a place like this? The red-blooded male inside him obviously thought she was perfect—but given that she was working on a house in the mountains all by herself, he couldn't deny the likelihood that there might be something strange going on with her.

Especially when calling this cabin a *house* was...generous. The floor and walls were bare except for a standing kitchen sink, a makeshift wooden counter to hold a microwave and a laptop, a couple of boxes on the floor filled with kitchen paraphernalia, an air bed in the corner by the wood stove, one sling chair, and a camp stove. The kitchen itself was missing both appliances and cabinetry. The only convenience besides the sink was a mini-fridge that would fit milk and yogurt and not much more.

"The fireplace was starting to crumble, so I put in a wood-burning stove that keeps the place nice and toasty." She flourished her hand as if she were showing him an array of sparkling diamonds.

She'd done a surprisingly good job tearing out the

old stone and installing a large wood-burner with a sensible catalytic converter. It would heat the kitchen and family room, with a hint of warmth for the bedroom too.

Noticing his glance at the air mattress, she toed it with her booted foot. "It's surprisingly comfortable, and it's even got its own pump. The only problem is that when it's cold, the air inside goes cold too, so I have to pile as many blankets underneath me as I do on top of me. Which is why I dragged it in here." She gave a nod to the bedroom. "Also because there's a couple of holes in the floor in there—well, maybe more than a couple." She gave him a sheepish grin. "I didn't want to break an ankle in the middle of the night."

Her voice was like a shower of music over him, and he didn't say anything in order to keep her talking.

She twirled in the middle of the room, her arms out. "I put up insulation and Sheetrock on the inside because you could see right through the wood siding in places, where the wind whistled through at night. It needs taping and texturing, of course, and then I can paint it," she added, as though embarrassed at the bareness of the Sheetrock. "And some of the floorboards were rotting, so I replaced those. But I'd really like to lay down a proper subfloor and hardwood. Or laminate."

"Hardwood," he suggested, though she hadn't asked for his opinion.

She was completely animated now, showing him

her accomplishments, pride bringing a rose blush to her cheeks. Despite his initial impression that the place was a dump, after her mini-tour, he was amazed by everything she'd done, seemingly by herself.

"Where'd you learn how to do all this?"

She pointed to a laptop. "YouTube videos and do-it-yourself shows. It's amazing what you can learn on the Internet. I figured out how to install a toilet and a new shower, plus a vanity and sink. I just have to do the tiling. Then of course, there's the kitchen. And the roof. But I need to wait for more consistently sunny weather before I tackle that."

"You did all this yourself? From scratch, without knowing a thing?"

"Well, yeah. I don't watch just one video before I start a new project. I view a bunch, because everyone has different techniques. When you combine them all, everything works like magic."

Her smile knocked him sideways. Again.

"Do you want to see my toilet?" She pointed behind her to an open door just outside the bedroom. She was already backing toward it, her eager gaze tugging him.

He laughed, something he couldn't remember doing with a woman he was attracted to in, well, long enough that he simply couldn't remember. "A woman asking if I want to see her toilet is definitely a first."

She clapped her hand over her mouth, her words muffled behind her palm. "Oops. Sorry. I didn't think about it. It's just been so long since—" As if he'd waved a magic wand to put her to sleep, something shuttered in her eyes.

Wishing he'd kept his damned mouth shut, he said, "I'd love to see the toilet."

She didn't laugh, didn't even smile. "That's okay. I'm sure you're busy. And it's enough that you helped me off the roof. You don't have to be wowed by every single nail I've hammered too."

But he wanted to know what she'd been about to say before she caught herself. Yes, she was far from the perfect woman he'd been wishing for an hour earlier, but he still liked her enthusiasm, her excitement. "I'm working on my own cabin down the hill from you. It would be good to see how you're approaching things."

Before she could turn him down again, he side-stepped her to check out the bathroom. She'd installed a standard porcelain floor-mount next to a neat vanity with a wood bowl sink, its faucets and fixtures gleaming. The shower was a free-standing, European-style corner unit that he'd recommended on his show, with the drain in the floor.

"It looks great," he said, meaning it.

"I'm going to put in a tile backsplash," she said softly, "with blue and green glass. I just have to figure out what paneling to use that won't clash with it."

"There's a style that looks like a log cabin if you're interested." He stocked it in his stores.

She tipped her head, considering it. "I could see

how it might work, but I really want the blue-green glass."

"You could still do that. Just leave space in the paneling." He tipped his head too, almost touching hers. "But I'd recommend doing the tile from wall to wall, not just over the vanity itself. Better continuity. Maybe if you have any drawings for what you're planning, I could show you exactly what I'm talking about?"

"Well," she said slowly, as though torn about taking him up on his offer, "I don't have any formal drawings. But there is a video that's pretty much in line with my plans."

"Great," he said, already heading over to her laptop before she could change her mind.

She typed in the name of the website, then scrolled down the page to the video she wanted to select. A beat later, his face filled her screen, his voice pumping out over the onboard speakers.

"Oh my God." She hit the pause button at a particularly unflattering moment, his open mouth and squinted eyes flash-frozen on the screen. "What did you say your name was?"

"I didn't. And you didn't say yours."

"You're not—" She pointed at the appalling freeze-frame.

"Daniel Spencer."

She gazed at him in horror. "Is that a *yes, that's me*, or just a *no, that's just some guy who happens to look and sound like me.*"

"Yes, that's me."

She groaned, covering her face with both hands. "I can't believe this. I've been watching you for hours and hours, and I still didn't recognize you." She peeked out from between her fingers. "In my defense, can I say that I've mostly just watched your hands in the videos to see what you're doing with the wood or tile or pipes?"

Nothing about her words should have made the cabin suddenly feel hot. But just thinking about her watching him—even if she really had been looking only at his hands—made the fire that had begun to burn inside of him the moment he'd pulled her against him on the ladder jump at least a dozen levels hotter.

Chapter Four

"Tell me your name," Daniel said in a low voice that made Tasha feel warm all over in ways Eric *never* had, "and we'll call it even."

"I'm Natasha, but everyone calls me Tasha." She hoped, with no little desperation, that he wouldn't ask for her last name. Daniel was in the building industry, and her father had been building a resort, so it wasn't impossible that he could connect the dots.

But her father hadn't planned to actually *build* anything, had he? So it was unlikely that the two of them would have crossed paths.

Still, her stomach tightened and twisted, as it had for months, because who knew how far her father's devious net had spread?

Thankfully, Daniel simply stuck out his hand and said, "Nice to meet you, Tasha."

His hand was large and warm, with the most delicious calluses. Work hands. Big, tough man hands.

She'd already been on the verge of overheating simply from being this close to him—even with his shirt on, she would have been fighting the urge to drool—and now the feel of him wrapped around her hand like a blanket.

Forcefully, she reminded herself that all of this— her feelings, her attraction, her chatter—was bad. Wrong. She was supposed to steer clear of people, stay far away from temptation.

Maybe if he'd been just an average Joe, she'd be fine right now. Although honestly, it felt so good just to talk to someone that she'd gone on and on about every little thing she'd done around the place.

She wished she could chalk up her wildly beating pulse and slight breathlessness to being halfway to giddy after her fall, then shocked all over again after being rescued by a gorgeous, chocolate-eyed Adonis. One standing so close that she could smell the scrumptious all-male scent of him. It made her lightheaded and tongue-tied.

How could she have failed to recognize him immediately? Then again, who would ever have thought *the* Daniel Spencer would rescue her off a pitched roof? A tall, dark, handsome, filthy-rich guy showing up on *her* falling-apart doorstep?

That was like the prince putting the glass slipper on Cinderella's foot and having it fit. It only happened in fairy tales.

The one thing Tasha knew for sure—the *only* thing she knew for sure anymore—was that her life was no fairy tale.

"You were going to show me…?" He pointed at his

face on the screen. "I'd really like to stop staring into my open mouth, if you don't mind."

Horrified all over again—she couldn't seem to do anything right today—she started to shut the lid on the laptop. "Never mind. It's not important."

"No. Please. Show me." He tapped the touchpad, and his gorgeous screen mouth started speaking again. His voice was as chocolaty as his eyes, making her bones melt and her legs turn to jelly.

Why did *he* have to be living in the mansion down below?

The problem was that she needed him gone at least as much as she was dying for him to stay. He was too much temptation for her to rejoin the world.

Heck, he'd be too much temptation even if he looked like Godzilla, which he most definitely didn't. It didn't help, of course, that his sexy male scent tantalized her. The fine hairs on her arms rose as though trying to reach out to him. She rubbed her hands up and down her skin, trying to settle herself down.

"This could definitely work for your bathroom," he said after he'd watched ten or so seconds of the video, "especially if you continue the tile over the toilet, like this."

As he traced the screen, she could almost feel him caressing her skin in gentle lines and circles. He turned, felling her with a smile that would either knock her dead, or make her heart start beating right out of her chest.

"I've got an app on the website where we can sketch it out."

We.

She loved the sound of *we*. Even if she hadn't been alone for over three months, she would have loved the sound of *we*. She'd always been a people person, always felt more energized after a great conversation or party than by a quiet evening in. And it felt terrific to have him in her house—the only home that had ever truly been hers. To talk to someone besides the squirrels and birds and herself. Plus, he was surprisingly good at listening.

But she was in exile. She was here to do penance. To atone for her sins.

Which meant she couldn't let herself feel all breathless and giggly and sexy around him. She most certainly couldn't fall for gorgeous billionaire Daniel Spencer.

Really, she reminded herself, she didn't even know him. What if the man seemed nice and helpful—but was really a secret ax murderer, or was running his company as a front for illegal activities?

She'd proven herself to be absolutely *terrible* at reading people's true characters and motives. For God's sake, this guy owned the biggest chain of home-improvement stores in the world. *And* he was on TV, too handsome for mere mortals. A celebrity. A rich guy. They always had their own agendas, didn't they? Okay, so there wasn't one single thing about him that screamed *ax murderer* or *money launderer* or even *snooty know-it-all.*

Then again, she hadn't thought her family could be any of those things either.

"The app is free," he added, as though he thought that was why she hadn't responded. "Would you like to download it?"

It struck her that he was *asking* what she wanted to do instead of *telling* her, the way her father would have done. Or Eric.

As if she were wiping her windshield clean, she deliberately scraped all those thoughts out of her mind. Or she would go stark crazy. Besides, Daniel would be gone soon, and then she'd have to settle back into her solitude.

For just this one teeny-tiny moment, she wanted to enjoy him for all she was worth and savor the memory for the endlessly quiet days and nights to come.

So she said, "Yes, please."

After he demonstrated how to use the app, she couldn't help raving. "That is so cool. I could even do the kitchen using this. Plus, I can test out the log cabin paneling you talked about." Maybe it wasn't right for her to be so excited about turning her vision for the cabin into reality, not when living in a dilapidated shack was supposed to be part of her penance for her family's con jobs. But after a lifetime of longing for a real home, she simply couldn't help herself. No more than she could keep herself from excitedly asking

Daniel, "Did you build this app yourself?"

"I told a designer exactly what I wanted." He gave her a half-smile that only made him look more gorgeous. "I'm pretty sure he hates my guts now. I'm damn picky."

"I would love to have built something like this for you." She spoke without thinking.

He raised his eyebrows. "You build apps?"

Silently cursing herself for her mistake, she said, "I'm a graphic designer. Or at least I was...until I moved up here." She waved her hand at the screen, trying to be nonchalant about it. "I used to develop websites and do interactive stuff like this."

He turned, their noses almost touching, and homed in on the one thing she hadn't wanted him to focus on. "Why did you come here? All alone. To renovate a cabin by yourself."

Her racing heart thudded to an abrupt halt. This was exactly why she needed to keep away from other people. If she hadn't been chattering on, he wouldn't have felt he could ask her such a pointed question. Now that he had, she would have to tell him the same thing she'd emailed to her friends before she headed off—not a lie, but not the complete and very difficult truth either.

"I hit a crossroads and needed to unplug from the rat race." Unplugging was something everyone always said they wanted to do, so thankfully, no one argued with it. The irony was that Tasha was someone who longed to be plugged in all the time, not to digital devices, but with other people. "I needed to learn to depend on myself and no one else."

"Well, you should definitely be proud of what you've accomplished." Again, he was far kinder than a billionaire needed to be. "How-to videos are practically my bread and butter, and yet I never knew anyone could get so much done simply from watching them."

"I also asked a lot of questions at the hardware store. So many that now the staff run in the opposite direction when they see me coming."

"None of my clerks had better do that." He was surprisingly stern. Gorgeously so. "You're exactly the kind of customer we want. Eager, willing to experiment, open to trying new things."

A blush crawled up her cheeks, despite her trying not to melt into a puddle at his feet. *Eager. Willing to experiment. Open to trying new things.* It was really hard to remind herself that he wasn't talking about sex.

He pushed the laptop toward her. "Show me your work. I'd love to see it."

She was so busy trying to shove her hormones down that it took her several beats to realize what he'd said. "Work? You want to see my work?"

"Maybe I could use you when I've got another project."

Three months ago, she would have leaped at the chance to work for Daniel Spencer and Top Notch DIY. It would have been a dream come true. So she had to force out the words, "Sorry, but I don't do that stuff anymore. I'm done with the rat race. I like it here in my own little cabin in the mountains. The simple life. No frills." She hoped she sounded convincing, because *most* of it was true. She really did like the mountains. She just missed her work, her friends, and talking to someone other than herself.

"Fair enough," he said as the screen went blank in front of him. "Hopefully, the app will help you put your simple life together just the way you want it. If you need extra tools, feel free to come down and borrow anything I've got." He pointed up. "About the roof—"

She cut him off before he could offer the moon and the stars as well. The nicer he was, the harder it became to remember why she didn't deserve nice things. "Thanks. I've got everything I need."

Except someone to talk to. Someone to watch the sunrise and the sunset. Someone who made her laugh. Someone with unruly curls she could run her fingers through and dark chocolate eyes to gaze into.

No, no, *no*. Daniel seemed great, but so had her father when he'd offered her the commission for the website, saying it would be so good for her career. He'd been doing her such a big favor, giving the project to *her* instead of a big, professional company. Giving her a chance. So caring, so altruistic.

When really, he'd just wanted someone who wouldn't ask a lot of questions. But he'd destroyed her career. Her name had been on that website. Her reputation had been damaged. Along with her heart.

She'd been blind to her father's faults all her life. And she'd been blinded by Eric's slick façade too. So how was she supposed to figure out if Daniel Spencer was really as great as he seemed—or if it was all just a big lie?

And if he *did* turn out to be great, that would be even worse in some ways, because then he should be with someone equally marvelous, rather than a woman who had the stink of a nasty con job all over her.

"Well, if you do find you're missing something, feel free to stop by." He hooked a thumb over his shoulder. "As I'm sure you can tell, I'm building my own cabin too."

"My place is a cabin," she countered. "Yours is a lakefront mansion."

"It didn't start out that way. But I want my family to visit, so I need to make room for all of them."

"You must have a pretty big family." Up until now, she'd only thought of him as one of the most eligible bachelors on the planet. A big family that he loved was a whole other—far too sweet—addition to his appeal.

His smile brought the sunshine right in through the window. "One sister, Mom, Dad. Four foster brothers and all the family they bring with them."

"You sound like you adore them."

His shrug was carefree and boyish. "The Mavericks aren't a bad bunch."

"The Mavericks?"

"That's what we called ourselves back in high school. Me and my foster brothers."

"I like it." She'd adored her friends too. But her family had moved so often that it was hard to keep in touch with everyone, and now it had become impossible to call any of them, because she could never return to her old life.

He nudged her arm with his elbow. "What about you? What about your family? How do they feel about you living all the way out here in"—he gestured to the holes in her floor and ceiling—"this?"

Her stomach took another nose dive, the way it did every time he asked one of his far too on-point questions. "I haven't seen them for a while," she said flatly. Drew and her father were lost to her.

"I'm sorry." His gaze was kind, as though he truly felt her pain.

No matter how desperate she was for company, no matter how nice he seemed, talking about her family was a devastating reminder that she couldn't trust her own instincts.

Standing abruptly, she said, "I should get back to work."

He was forced to stand too, backing away as though he was reluctant to go. Although maybe that was just her projecting onto him, given that she hated the thought of his leaving. Not just because she didn't want to be alone again—but because being with Daniel made her feel completely alive and energized. More than she'd ever felt in her life.

"Don't fall off any more roofs," he said. "You need someone here with you next time you head up there, and be sure to secure yourself too. I can help, if you'd like."

"Thanks, but I finished tacking down the tarps just before I slipped." She felt like an ungrateful wretch when he was being so nice, but if she didn't let him go now, she was afraid she'd drag him back inside, ply him with coffee, and force him to talk to her for hours and hours. Instead, she'd have to make do with his videos. And, honestly, even those would be a sweet treat she didn't deserve. Especially after meeting him…and liking him so much.

As the door closed behind him, she sank to the floor, leaning back against the wall of a house that felt emptier and quieter and colder than ever before. Because for a few minutes, when Daniel was there with her, it had felt like a real home.

* * *

Daniel was his mother's son through and through—he couldn't stop trying to aid lost souls. Through his company and with hammer in hand, he'd helped many single parents and youths-on-the-edge work through their issues and move toward a better future.

Tasha was clearly a lost soul. Why else would such a beautiful, obviously capable woman run away from her career to hide in the wilds of Tahoe in a run-down shack? What had caused the pain in her eyes that had materialized more than once during their conversation?

Barely an hour ago, Daniel had been wishing for a perfect woman. What he'd found instead was a prickly yet adorably talkative new neighbor.

One whose mysteries he couldn't help but want to unravel, even if getting involved with a woman who obviously had big problems was the very last thing he should do.

Chapter Five

Tasha opted for indoor work the next day. She was afraid Daniel would come back if he saw her outside and got worried that she might climb up on her roof again. An even more likely possibility was that she'd go running down if she caught a glimpse of him. Her self-control was barely hanging by a thread after tossing and turning all night on her freezing-cold air bed.

Any way she tried to turn Daniel over in her head, she couldn't make him into a bad guy. Everything about him screamed *helpful* and *kind* and *generous*.

Not to mention the fact that his bed, she was certain, would be cozy warm.

Especially with him in it.

"You cannot think about his bed," she chastised herself in a loud voice. "Or him working shirtless and getting all sweaty and—"

She groaned. She was so bad at this. Bad at ignoring her need to talk to another person. And also bad at ignoring other needs she'd sworn had died forever the day she'd learned what a fraud Eric was. Fortunately, thinking about her ex worked like a charm to erase the super-sexy visions dancing in her head.

Determined to make good headway, she got to work replacing the rotten boards in the bedroom. For the first fifteen minutes, everything went swimmingly. All she needed to do was keep herself from thinking about Daniel and how sweet and helpful he'd been yesterday and how much she'd wanted to—

The drill bit snapped in two.

"I'm cursed." All she'd done was *think* about Daniel and the bit had broken. It was karmic punishment, she was sure.

She grabbed her toolbox and rooted around for another bit, but she was clean out. Which meant a trip to the hardware store in town, thirty minutes away.

Or, the devil inside her head suggested wickedly, she could ask Daniel if he had a bit to spare.

She groaned, dropping her head in her hands.

"Everything going okay?"

She whipped around, almost tripping. The very man who was distracting her beyond reason stood in her roughly framed doorway. Arms crossed over his chest, he wore a lumberman's flannel shirt rolled up to the elbows and faded jeans that hugged every muscle.

Before she could reply—she was too busy drooling for her brain to work properly—he noticed the broken drill bit.

"I've got some extra bits if you need one."

"I do, actually."

"Great. I came to see if you wanted to share some

breakfast with me." He grinned, and for the life of her, she couldn't help grinning right back. "Fresh-baked doughnuts."

In other circumstances, she would have forced herself to say no. But she really did need that drill bit. And with all the conflicting thoughts and emotions roiling around inside her after he'd left her yesterday, she hadn't been able to face food either last night or this morning.

Still, she reminded herself as they walked the short distance down the mountain to his house, she needed to make it absolutely clear—to herself even more than to him—that she wouldn't stay any longer than it took to grab the drill bit and stuff a doughnut in her mouth.

But as she walked into his house, all of her resolutions disappeared. "Wow. This is amazing."

She wanted to stay forever.

The massive room stretched from the front door to wall-to-wall windows overlooking a huge deck and stone fire pit, with a view of sparkling water and snow-drenched mountains. The great room had a twelve-foot pitched ceiling with open beams that loomed above her and a magnificent stone fireplace dominating an angled wall built specifically for it. The interior rooms were divided by log walls, and through an archway cut in the logs, she could see the space for a dining room and kitchen.

Right now, it contained only a small fridge, plus a microwave and coffee machine on a cart big enough for a cutting board and a cabinet underneath. But she could see what his home would become—and it was breathtaking.

As breathtaking as its owner.

He showed her the guest bedrooms, plus a game room large enough for a pool table, then the master suite with a sitting area in front of the huge windows and another fireplace, which had a flue but no stonework yet.

She stopped in her tracks when she saw the bed—the very bed she'd daydreamed about. Only, her daydreams had nothing on this masterpiece. It was a ginormous sleigh bed, its wood polished and gleaming in the light falling through the ceiling-high windows.

"What do you think?"

He had to be asking her if she liked the house, but when he was standing this close and smelling so good, it was nearly impossible to think about anything other than pulling back the wine-dark counterpane covering the thick mattress and dragging him down with her into the middle of all that softness.

"It's great," she said. The world's biggest understatement.

With that, she hurried down the hall, away from the warm deliciousness of the way he made her feel. Away from the temptation to make another huge mistake.

Because she could, with him. The last thing anyone needed was to get involved with a train wreck like her—especially a man as high-profile as Daniel.

"It's all so big," she added as she made a wrong turn and ended up in the game room.

"I didn't intend to make the house this large when I started out," he said as he led her back to the stairs.

She took them on shaky legs. No man had ever made her feel like this, not even Eric, with whom she'd foolishly thought she was in love.

"But I needed to add an extra bedroom for my parents," he continued, "then one for my sister. And all the Mavericks. And now I need more rooms because my friends have all made their own additions to the family with wives and girlfriends and kids and mothers-in-law."

His smile, full of joy and love and pride, spoke of how much he cared. As much as she had once cared for her family. As much as she still did, even though she knew better.

The sadness hit so fast, her heart felt like it was tearing in two—one half for Drew, one half for her father. If things had been normal, she would have asked Daniel more about Noah and Matt and Jeremy and all the other Maverick family he'd mentioned while they toured the house. But nothing was normal anymore.

Nothing would ever be normal again.

Furiously working to blink back tears she didn't dare let Daniel see—if she cried in front of him, he'd ask questions, and then she'd have to flat-out lie to him while fighting the urge to spill her guts—she pointed at the fireplace. "You could roast an elephant in there." Thank God her voice didn't wobble. "I love the way the river rock climbs all the way up the wall. Did you do all this yourself?" She held up her hands, turning in a circle to indicate the entire amazing house.

"My friends helped me put the roof and log frame in place, but everything was cut to order, so all we had to do was lay it out. The rest has pretty much been a one-man job that I work on when I need to get away from the office. I'm actually keeping everyone out except the guys until it's done." He said it like he was a kid building a fort out in the backyard who wouldn't let his parents see till it was all done—rather than a billionaire who was building the world's most beautiful waterfront mansion.

"But you're letting me see it?"

"You have a good eye, Tasha." He smiled at her again. "And I'm really glad we're neighbors."

The flattery she felt at his compliment dried up in an instant. If he knew what she'd been party to—the scams her family had pulled on unsuspecting people all over the country—he wouldn't be glad that she was in the next house over. On the contrary, he'd probably pull strings to get her kicked out of the county.

Her heart thumping hard inside her chest, she said, "Thanks for showing me around, but I should probably just grab the drill bit and leave you to your work."

"What about doughnuts and coffee?"

Her stomach growled at the offer of sugar and caffeine, giving her away, but she needed to remain firm. Resolute. She hadn't come to the mountains to snare a sexy billionaire—she'd come to figure out how she could have made so many mistakes in both her personal and professional lives, and ensure she never made them again.

Besides, she could only imagine the way her father would try to take advantage of Daniel and his generous nature if he ever found out his daughter knew the billionaire.

The thought made her tremble with dread. "I really should get back to work. The holes in my floor aren't going to close themselves."

"If you need help, I can take a break," he offered. "There's no time limit on getting this place done since I'm not actually living here."

She made herself back away. It was easier this time, with her gut burning a crater at the images of her father taking advantage of Daniel. "I'm fine, really. Perfectly comfortable. I've got everything I need."

"Except a roof that doesn't leak and an insulated subfloor and a decent meal." Damn him for pointing out so many incontrovertible facts. "Why don't you come for dinner tonight? I do a mean barbecue."

She wanted to leap on him and shout, *Yes, yes, yes!* Instead, she said, "I can't tonight," even though they both knew she'd be shivering over her camp stove while picking at canned beans and soggy hot dogs.

He stared at her for a long moment. She held her breath. Would he insist, or would he let her run away to her ruin of a house?

Finally, he turned to fish through a huge rolling tool chest with multiple drawers containing screws, nuts, bolts, and nails. He came up with a bit that matched her broken one. "Here you go."

Disappointment speared her that he'd let her off the hook so easily. Despite the fact that this was exactly what she needed him to be—just a friendly neighbor with an extra drill bit.

And nothing more.

★ ★ ★

Daniel stood in his open doorway watching Tasha trudge back up the hill, his drill bit shoved deep in her overalls pocket. He itched to run after her, help her— even just to feed her something more edible than beans and hot dogs. She was fiercely independent, which made her captivatingly different from the women he dated. At the same time, she harbored too many secrets, obviously shutting herself down whenever she thought she might be revealing too much.

Daniel's idea of a perfect relationship was total openness, no questions necessary, complete trust—all the reasons his parents had such a great marriage.

And yet...he'd never felt so drawn to a woman. He wanted to know everything about Tasha, to plumb her depths. She was talented, intelligent, and industrious.

Only someone completely special could have accomplished the things she had all on her own. Unconsciously attractive, she seemed unaware of her own loveliness. And he had to admit he was a sucker for a woman who knew her way around a tool chest and a hammer.

The guys would laugh him off the planet with that one, even though they would understand.

Daniel watched until she disappeared around the corner of her ramshackle cabin at the precise moment that his phone rang. He smiled when his mom's name appeared on the screen.

"Hey, pretty lady." He strolled through the house to the back deck, flopping down in a chair with his phone at his ear.

"Hi, honey. Tell me how you're getting along on the cabin. Your father and I are dying to see your rustic retreat."

He laughed, thinking of what Tasha had said. "Actually, it's turning out to be a bit more than just a vacation cabin. But I'm still hoping to finish it by the end of the summer." And thinking about Tasha made him realize how much he'd look forward to coming up here, oh, just about every weekend. "In fact, I see spending a lot of time here in my future."

"Oh, you do?" He could picture his mom's raised brow. "And, pray tell, is there a special reason for that?"

He'd never been coy with his mother. So even though he hadn't quite made up his mind about his feelings for Tasha, he said, "I met a woman. She bought the cabin up the hill." He crossed his booted feet and propped them on the railing, settling back.

"Ah, a new mountain neighbor. Smart and funny?"

"Gorgeous and talented too." He told his mom all the things Tasha had done around her place. "And she loves my DIY videos."

His mother laughed. "Goodness, you need to snap this paragon right up. She sounds perfect for you."

He sobered. "That's the problem."

"That she's a paragon?"

He closed his eyes, letting the sun warm him while he pictured Tasha's smile—it would flash so brightly one moment, and then be gone the next. "Something just isn't adding up. Why is she up here all alone trying to fix a cabin that should clearly be scrapped and rebuilt from the foundation up? Why did she leave a good job as a graphic designer to retrofit a dive?" He shrugged as if his mother could see him. "She doesn't even have a cell phone, as far as I can tell."

"Your father and I lived perfectly well without a cell phone for most of our lives," his mother pointed out.

"It's not about the cell phone," he said. "I just get the feeling there's more to her story. That there might be a whole bunch of messy stuff surrounding her and her life."

"You know, honey, I've never heard you talk about a woman this much, messy or not." His mother seemed hopeful that he would soon meet his match the way the other Mavericks had. "Maybe you should give it a little more time and pursue getting to know her better. You might find the mess isn't as bad as you think."

"In my experience, it's usually a helluva lot worse. And you know that I've always steered clear of messy relationships."

"I do know that, honey. But sometimes, waiting for perfection can be just a way of avoiding mistakes. If you never make a mistake, you never take the risk of finding exactly what you're looking for. In fact," she said in a slightly softer voice, "messes are usually a part of even the very best relationships."

"Not for you and Dad," he countered. "You're the all-time-perfect love story."

He waited for her to agree with him, but when she remained silent, he continued. "I like Tasha. And I won't deny that I'm drawn to her. But I'm also not willing to settle for less than the perfect love that you and Dad have always shared with each other."

Again, his mother remained conspicuously silent. Until finally she said, "Every relationship has its bumps, even if no one but the couple ever knows about them. And sometimes..."

He waited for her to finish, but she'd gone quiet on him again, halfway through a sentence.

Frowning, he prompted, "Mom? Is everything okay?"

"Of course it is," she said in a voice that sounded a little too bright. "We were talking about Tasha, weren't we? So...I think..."

She fumbled for words. Even though his mother never fumbled. She always had the right thing to say at the right time. All the guys knew that. She was their relationship guru.

"Mom, if this is a bad time, we can talk later."

"Sure," she said quickly. "Let's do that. I should go. Keep me updated. Love you, hon. Bye."

Okay, that was strange. Really strange.

Daniel stared at the ripples sparkling on the lake, his brow scrunched. If something was bugging him, he invariably felt boosted after talking with his mom.

Except today. Maybe she was just having a bad day.

Only, she never had bad days.

It was almost like she'd been talking about bumps in *her* relationship. But that couldn't be. His parents *never* had bumps. It wasn't possible.

This was how much his feelings for Tasha had thrown him—he'd even started to doubt his parents' relationship. Clearly, he needed to figure out a way to get his head on straight.

Only, with Tasha so near, he had a feeling that wasn't going to be easy.

Chapter Six

"Daniel." His name trilled through the trees like birdsong. "I need you."

He'd been dreaming of Tasha all night, sexy visions of threading his fingers into her silky black hair while she whispered her secrets to him in the dark of the night. Everything he wanted to know about her, every part of her he wanted to touch.

He pulled the covers higher, trying to sink deeper into his fantasies.

"Daniel." He felt a hand on his shoulder, one that couldn't possibly be part of a dream.

Opening his eyes, he found Tasha standing beside his bed wearing her overalls and another baseball cap, this one proclaiming her to be a *T-Rex Whisperer*.

Still half asleep, he nearly reached out to tumble her into bed with him, just like his dream, and rescue her from any big, bad T-rex chasing her—or let her rescue him. Oh yeah, he liked that idea. He might have done exactly that if he hadn't finally processed the worried expression on her face.

"I'm so sorry to barge into your house like this,"

she said. "But I yelled and yelled. Then I noticed your door was unlocked. Honestly, I would never do anything like this except..." She bit her lip, looking so damn kissable. "I really need your help."

The fear in her voice brought him fully awake. He shoved back the covers to bound out of bed, when he remembered at the last second that he not only had nothing on, but also his fantasies about Tasha meant she'd be getting a *serious* eyeful.

"Sorry," she said again, her eyes huge as she took in his bare chest and hips and the happy trail that continued beneath the corner of the sheet he'd managed to keep over himself. "I wasn't thinking. I just needed your help. But I should have thought you'd be...undressed." She flushed a deep rose, then spun on her heel, putting her back to him. "I'll wait downstairs."

Sixty seconds later, he was jogging down the stairs, jeans and boots on, buttoning his flannel shirt. "What's wrong?"

"I was hiking when I found puppies." Of everything he'd thought she'd say, *puppies* was nowhere on the list. "I heard something crying, and once I figured out where it was coming from, I shone the small flashlight I always carry with me into the little cave, but there was no way I could get to them. I counted three, their little eyes blinking and open mouths wailing at me. I didn't see the mother anywhere. If we don't get them out..." She swallowed hard, and he could see her fears bubbling up. "We *have* to get them out, Daniel."

"We will." Without seeing the cave, he had no idea how difficult it would be, but he'd move heaven and earth to erase that scared look from Tasha's eyes. "We'll need a strong flashlight and a shovel," he said, thinking out loud.

"And towels, so we can wrap them up to keep them warm. There's still snow on the ground up there."

After quickly grabbing everything, they headed out, with Tasha running up the mountain to the ridge behind her cabin. She didn't pant at the pace she'd set, pushing through brambles without a thought for the scratches they left on her arms, dodging tree trunks that got in her way, leaping over fallen logs. She didn't falter even as five minutes turned to ten of full-out, uphill sprinting.

Suddenly, she dropped to her knees before a jumble of fallen logs. "Here they are." She tossed aside the towel and handed him the flashlight.

He heard the cries, a series of pitiful mewls emanating from a hole dug out beneath the branches. Lying on his side, he shone the light. Three sets of eyes glittered in the beam.

The creatures were quiet a moment, blinking at him, until they all opened their mouths at once in a cacophony of pathetic puppy howls. He could make out black muzzles and tan bodies.

"I'll see if I can reach them." Unfortunately, the

moment he reached in, the poor things shrieked in terror and huddled deeper into the small cavern. He glanced back over his shoulder. "We can probably move the logs to get them out."

"I tried." Her hands were stained with dirt, her nails torn, her face streaked with sweat. Amazingly, she was more beautiful than ever. "We have to do *something*. They probably haven't eaten. They could be starving."

Daniel strained to move the logs, but she was right. Time and the elements had turned the mud between the logs into mortar, creating a perfect home for rabbits and other wild things.

Meanwhile, Tasha hadn't wasted any time grabbing the shovel and climbing over the tangle of rotting wood to start digging. He recognized a spark in her that reminded him of his mother—that selflessness, that willingness to run as fast and as far as she could for some poor, trapped animals. Their cries had brought tears to her eyes.

He wanted to take the shovel from her, but Tasha's generosity wasn't the only thing he identified. His mother had never been afraid of hard work. She'd never categorized tasks as men's work versus women's work. She'd always expected everyone to pitch in, whether they were cleaning toilets, cooking dinner, or chopping wood.

Bumps. The word came at him, a word he'd been deliberately ignoring since yesterday's conversation with his mother. *Every relationship has its bumps, even if no one but the couple ever knows about them.*

Daniel shook his mother's words out of his head— he didn't have time to start analyzing her strange comments again. Not now. The important thing was helping Tasha rescue the puppies.

He moved to the other side of the logs, taking the towels with him. "I'll stand over here in case they hear the noise and get scared enough to run out this way." He wanted to do the digging for her, but she was so intense, so fierce, he realized she needed to do it herself.

"Good idea," Tasha said, slamming the spade into the earth. "I wonder if they were abandoned by their owners. Or brought up here from the city and dumped."

"Who would do that?" Daniel asked, even though he knew full well how evil people could be. "Drop off puppies in the wilderness just because you don't want to take them to an animal shelter?"

The look she leveled on him was pained. "People can be thoughtless and cruel." She turned back to dig with renewed vigor, until she finally said, "I think I've got it!" The hole was now wide enough for her to lie on the ground and wriggle her arm and most of her torso inside. "I can see the light shining through," she called to him. "Can you reach them?"

"They're coming back your way." His voice echoed between them over the puppies' increasingly frantic mewls.

"Okay, I can just about reach one of them." Her side of the hole darkened. "Yes, yes, I've got him!" Triumph sparkled through her voice.

Daniel reached for another that had been backing away from Tasha's questing hand, locked onto its soft scruff, and pulled it out. The poor little mite cried, but didn't squirm, as though it didn't have enough energy to put up a fight. "I've got another one," he called to her over the tangle of logs.

"They're so skinny. And weak. And cold." She sounded utterly heartbroken as she curled the towel around the small, shivering bundle in her arms.

"Take this one too, and I'll try to get the last one out."

She carefully bundled both puppies together in the towel, holding them against her chest. "It's okay, little ones," she crooned. "You're going to be okay. We'll take care of you. We won't let anything happen to you."

She hadn't wanted his tools or his help to fix her house, but she was willing to beg him to save these poor little puppies. Put some helpless animals in front of her, and she threw everything aside to rescue them.

He squirmed as far into the hole as he could, but the last puppy backed in the opposite direction, terrified of the big intruder. "I can't do it without you," he called through the hole.

"Let me set these two little ones down. I don't

think they're going to run away. They seem too exhausted."

A moment later, her flashlight beamed against the dirt walls and floated across the tiny body huddled between them. It cried in terror, backing away from Tasha's searching fingers...and right into Daniel's waiting grip.

He dug into the scruff and pulled the little guy out. "Got it."

"Let's make a burrito-style wrap for them," Tasha suggested. With the dogs safely wrapped, she cuddled them close. "Look at them. They can't stop trembling."

She swiped at her face, and Daniel realized it wasn't dirt she was wiping away but tears. Her mouth wobbly, she looked at him with damp, brilliantly blue eyes.

"Thank you. I couldn't have gotten them out on my own. They might have died in there."

"They're going to be fine." He touched her cheek, drying the last streak of a tear, his heart feeling too big in his chest as he gazed down at her. "And you don't need to thank me. We work well together."

She nodded, then leaned into him for a brief second. "Everything's going to be okay now," she whispered.

He couldn't help but wonder—was she talking to the puppies?

Or was she trying to convince herself that everything was going to be okay in her life too?

★ ★ ★

While Daniel canvassed their neighbors about the puppies' missing mother, then took a trip into town for dog food, Tasha fashioned a crate for them out of the carton her mini-fridge had come in.

Daniel had wanted to take the puppies to his house, but she couldn't stand the thought of letting them out of her sight until she knew they were well again. "You've got too much space for them to scamper around in. I'm afraid they'll get lost."

"You've got holes in your floor they could fall through," he pointed out.

"Not anymore. I fixed them all once I had your drill bit."

She didn't mean to be a pain in the butt after everything he'd done to help her—but she couldn't afford to be traipsing down to Daniel's place to see the puppies. She would end up spending *all* her time down there, and that would create an impossible situation.

Especially after that spectacular view of him in his bedroom. Her face still burned with embarrassment at the memory, but her heart was also beating deliriously fast. His naked chest, all those muscles, that arrow of hair disappearing down into the sheets.

Oh yes, *everything* got hot remembering that.

All the more reason she simply couldn't be flitting down to see the puppies. These little creatures were all that mattered, not her forbidden thoughts about what

Daniel looked like naked under his sheet.

When she and Daniel had brought the puppies into the cabin, they hadn't run around investigating the way normal animals would have. Half starved and still shivering, they'd barely moved at all. After drinking some water, they'd fallen asleep in the makeshift crate, wrapped up in a bed of clean shop rags and hand towels.

Tossing her ball cap, which had become filthy with all the digging and crawling, Tasha sat cross-legged on the floor, her arm draped over the side of the box. "Don't worry, we've got food on the way, and you're going to be just fine. I won't let anything happen to you." She stroked each head in turn, giving comfort and warmth.

"Puppy Chow," Daniel said from the open doorway. Seeing that the puppies were sleeping, he lowered his voice to a loud whisper as he sauntered in to set a large bag of dog food on the kitchen counter. "How are they doing?" He knelt beside her.

She couldn't have rescued the puppies without him. And he hadn't been the slightest bit annoyed over the work time he'd lost. He'd even rushed all the way to town for food and seen whether anyone in the neighborhood knew about a pregnant dog that matched the puppies' description.

What better knight in shining armor could a girl—or three little puppies—ask for?

"They don't even have the energy to move or stay

awake." Her voice quavered with worry. "Are you sure we should give them regular puppy food to start? What if they can't digest it?"

"Let's try it once they wake up, then we can see how they do and adjust from there. I called the local vet for an appointment, but they're completely slammed today, and unless we want to drive an hour into Carson City, the earliest they can see them is tomorrow."

The runt of the litter whined and snorted, as if its tummy was rumbling even as it slept. Daniel reached in to soothe the little one with a stroke over its furry body.

He was good with animals. With women too, she guessed, certain he must have an amazing girlfriend, or else a string of beautiful women he could be with any time he liked.

"I'm so glad you know what you're doing." She was wistful. "I had a cat once when I was a kid, but I couldn't keep it."

"Why?"

"My family moved so much that it wasn't practical to have an animal."

That was the excuse her father always gave. Now she knew the truth—he couldn't run as fast with an animal in tow. She was surprised he'd ever had kids. Odds were, she suddenly thought, that she and Drew had been mistakes. She couldn't remember her mother, who'd died of a ruptured appendix when Tasha was only three. Would they have stayed in one place longer and had a real home if her mother hadn't died? And had her mother known that her husband was crooked?

Tasha tamped down her bitter thoughts. "What about you?"

"No pets. My parents could barely afford to feed all the kids they took in."

"Oh wow. I had no idea—" She squashed the insensitive words.

"I wasn't born with money," he said, answering the question she had no business asking. "Far from it."

"Your parents sound wonderful." While her father had been swindling money out of as many people as he could, Daniel's parents had been busy taking in foster kids even though they didn't have enough themselves.

He continued to stroke the puppies. "Yeah. They're amazing."

It was how she used to feel about her family. And how she would never feel again. At least not for her father. If only she knew how involved Drew had been. Had he been a reluctant partner? Had their father threatened him with something?

She realized Daniel was staring into space, frowning, as though *amazing* was only part of his mother and father's story. She couldn't help but wonder about the things he wasn't telling her. Not that he owed her any explanations, of course, especially given that she wasn't about to offer any information about herself.

"Why'd you move so much?" Daniel asked.

The question jolted her yet again. "My father's job."

"Was he in the military?"

"Investments." Hating herself for leaving off the word *fraudulent*, she quickly changed the subject. "Did you find out anything about the puppies' mother from the neighbors?"

Though he raised an eyebrow at her quick conversational shift, he answered, "No missing pregnant dogs and no one's seen one wandering around. Not even a stray."

"Something must have happened to her. A mother would never leave her babies alone and unprotected like that." Though her father certainly hadn't protected Tasha or her brother, had he? "We'll just have to figure out how to feed them." She jumped up to grab her laptop. "There's got to be some information online that will help."

At that moment, the fattest guy in the bunch—which wasn't saying much since they were all clearly malnourished—woke and started to howl.

Daniel picked him up, cradling him in his muscled arms. It was enough to make her heart turn over. "Time to fill that belly of yours." He scratched the puppy's tummy until it quieted into soft snuffles and snorts, falling completely under his spell.

As Tasha watched them together, she realized that the puppy wasn't the only one who had lost his heart to the gorgeous, and very sweet, billionaire.

Chapter Seven

"Here's something." Tasha pointed to the website she'd found. "It says to soften the Puppy Chow with milk. And go easy on the amount of food at first so they don't make themselves sick."

"Let's give it a try." Daniel carried the puppy to the counter while Tasha broke into the bag, added milk along with the kibble to a bowl, and microwaved it for a few seconds to soften it.

The machine dinged, and after she made sure it was cool enough, they set the puppy on the counter in front of the bowl. He sniffed, whined, unsure.

Daniel scooped a dab onto his finger, and the puppy licked it clean, then wanted more. "That's a good boy. Eat up." After a few more licks off Daniel's finger, he chowed down in the bowl, wolfing the food like he hadn't had a meal in forever.

"I wonder how long they've been alone?" Tasha asked.

Daniel mixed up another two bowls. "Couldn't be too long, or they would have died of dehydration in that hole. A full-grown dog can go maybe three days."

He frowned. "But puppies?"

While Tasha cradled the sated puppy, Daniel knelt by the makeshift crate, murmuring softly to the other two.

There was something incredibly moving about watching a big, strong man be so tender with a tiny, helpless animal. His caring shone through. Men with animals were like men with babies—enough to make her eyes tear up.

But with Daniel it was more. Considering how wealthy he was, he could have been high-and-mighty. He could have called in a minion—she was sure he had dozens of employees—to shunt the puppies off to the pound. But he'd scrounged around inside that hole himself to rescue them, driven into town for food, and trudged door to door to talk to the neighbors.

In many ways, his kindness made him far more dangerous than if he'd been a self-obsessed jerk.

It was one thing to give up something she didn't want.

It was another entirely to have to turn away from a man like Daniel.

Tasha studied the strong lines of his face, the laugh creases at his eyes, the smile curving his mouth. She wanted to touch him to make sure he was real, but by now, in the aftermath of their puppy rescue mission, she was absolutely sure there wasn't a single phony thing about him.

If only she could say the same about herself, but

her life had been a lie. Even now, while she was supposed to be alone in the mountains atoning for her family's sins and all the people they'd hurt, she was mooning over a sexy, handsome, rich man.

"Come on, little guy." Daniel's voice was soft and coaxing as the middle puppy stuck its face in a bowl, getting the food all over its muzzle in its haste to gulp down the gruel. But the smallest one barely moved.

Daniel picked it up, trying to get it to stand, only to have it collapse immediately.

"Do you have a spoon?" he asked Tasha. "I think he needs to be hand-fed."

"*He* is actually a *she*." Tasha stroked the biggest one still in her arms. "Boy." Then she pointed at the one currently wolfing down food. "Another boy." And finally to the poor little mite who could barely stand. "Girl. And yes, I have a spoon." With her free hand, she fumbled through her cutlery box on the floor and came up with a small jam-pot spoon she'd found at a thrift store.

Daniel spooned a smidgen, trying to get the little puppy to take it, but she didn't even open her mouth.

"I've got an idea." Tasha grabbed one of the hand towels she'd laid in the crate. "Let's wrap her in the burrito bundle like we did when we carried them home. Holding her on her back like a baby might make her feel more comfortable."

"Great suggestion. The big and medium guys didn't seem to have any problems, thankfully." After a moment, he added, "You know what? They need better names than the big one, the medium one, and the runt."

The thought of naming them made Tasha a little queasy. Already, she wanted to keep them forever. She could too easily imagine the fun they would have together once the puppies were fattened up. Three furry companions who would make all the difference in her life. Who would make this place a true home. As it was, just having Daniel here make her shack feel like home.

"Larry, Curly, and Moe," Daniel suggested as he rolled the tiny female in his arms. Her eyes remained pathetically closed.

"You watched *The Three Stooges*?"

He put a spoonful of mashed food to the puppy's mouth, obviously hoping the scent would tempt her. "Saturday mornings when I was kid, on whatever stations we could get from our old antenna, we watched reruns of all the old shows. Wile E. Coyote, the Marx Brothers."

This magnificent man had grown up poor, without even cable TV. Whereas she'd had every channel known to man. Courtesy of stolen money.

"How about Heckle, Jeckle, and Hyde?" he asked when she didn't agree to his first recommendation. Just then, a little pink tongue finally flicked out and licked at the spoon. "There you go, Heckle."

"That's a terrible name for a puppy." But Tasha still

laughed, loving the name game. "How about Groucho, Harpo, and Chico?" she said, even though she knew her suggestions weren't much better than his had been.

"They don't look like the Marx Brothers," he argued. "And she deserves a more feminine name." He rocked the puppy, who was at last eating every bite he offered.

Tasha laid the big boy in the box, where he rolled over to sleep.

Daniel came up with another idea. "All right then, how about Froggy, Spanky, and Darla?"

She picked up the medium puppy and he too immediately fell asleep, starting to snore softly, his breathing raspy through his open mouth. "You know what?" She smiled, aware that she was happier than she had any right to be. "I think we've got a winner."

★ ★ ★

Daniel's stomach growled as the smallest bundle fell into a deep sleep in his arms, finally sated. "All right, this one is Darla. That guy"—he pointed at the one in Tasha's arms—"is Froggy." The relatively fat puppy suddenly yowled in the box. "And he's Spanky, because he's always hungry."

"Honestly," Tasha said, "that sounded more like your stomach than Spanky's."

"Come on down to my place. I've got some sandwich fixings."

Anticipation flashed in her eyes, but just as quickly,

it was gone. She set Froggy in the box, and once Daniel put Darla in there too, Spanky stopped in mid-yowl and flopped over, succumbing to the warmth of his brother and sister and once again falling asleep.

"Thanks for the offer." She was already rising, and he heard the *but* before she said it. "But I've got a can of soup I was planning to heat up."

She was such a strange—and beautiful—creature. Open and laughing one minute, closed in on herself the next. Almost as though she thought it was wrong to be happy, bad to feel joy, and needed to constantly shut it down, no matter how difficult it might be to hide away the naturally sunny part of herself.

Instinctively, he knew there was more to her story. But what was it?

And should he even try to find out?

He'd waited thirty-six years to find the perfect soul mate, someone without shadows or secrets, someone totally open, so that he could have the same amazing marriage as his parents. Only, he hadn't known about any *bumps* then, had he?

His parents had been totally committed to each other since forever, so what kind of bumps could they possibly have encountered? It had to be way more than money problems...

Frustrated, he said, "Soup sounds great," even though Tasha hadn't actually offered him any.

"It's tomato." She said it in a flat voice, obviously trying to make the soup sound as unappetizing as possible.

"I love tomato soup."

"*Nobody* loves tomato soup." She retrieved a can from a box on the microwave. "I only bought it because it was on sale."

He couldn't think of the last time a woman had tried to kick him out. He'd always been the one trying to figure out how to leave. Now, all he wanted was to stay, even though his rule had always been: Don't get involved in messes.

Yet here he was getting more and more involved with Tasha, and the mystery of her, with each passing day.

"Bet you're regretting not letting me have the puppies at my place, aren't you?" He moved closer, until he could smell the outdoors and the dirt and the puppies on her. Nothing had ever been more erotic. "Now you can't get rid of me."

Her mouth moved until she was biting down on her bottom lip, clearly trying to keep whatever she was dying to say from leaping out of her mouth.

"Come on," he whispered, the hair at her nape ruffling with his breath. "Admit it."

Her chin trembled. He wanted to stroke his finger along her lower lip.

Suddenly, she laughed, shoving at him with her elbow in his stomach. "Yes, I'm totally regretting it—I can't even open a can of soup without you getting in the way."

He liked her feistiness. He liked her laughter too. Mom and Dad would love her. Daniel had no doubt they'd get the dirt on her secrets in no time.

But what about his parents—did they have secrets? And if so, did he really want to know them? Was it even his business?

Tasha held out a can and the opener. "If you're going to stay, make yourself useful."

"I *was* useful," he reminded her, not above using a little puppy love to his advantage. "I helped get those three furballs to safety."

She stopped, her two hands against his chest, one with the opener, the other holding the can. "Jumping out of bed to run up the hill and dig them out. Getting the food. Canvassing the neighbors. Feeding them." Her words were slightly rough with emotion. "You've gone above and beyond."

He couldn't help but pull her close, couldn't stop himself from wrapping his arms around her, holding her tight. "So have you," he whispered into her hair as he gently stroked her back.

She stayed there for five seconds, a heaven's length of time in which he absorbed every curve, every texture, every scent.

Especially since he knew it wouldn't last. Not yet. Not until she trusted him with whatever it was that kept sending those shadows into her eyes.

But just as he'd thought about his parents' secrets, did he really want to know Tasha's? Or would it be safer to keep his distance and wait for *perfect* and *uncomplicated* to come along?

Deep within himself, Daniel knew better. Knew that what he felt for Tasha, even after only a couple of days, was special.

Even if it wasn't quite perfect.

Just as he'd known she would, Tasha sprang away from him. As she clutched the soup can and opener to her chest, her eyes were wide, her gaze full of something that looked a heck of a lot like self-recrimination. Just because she'd let him hug her.

He wanted to say something that would soothe her—and make up for the huge gaffe of pulling her too close, too soon—but he had a feeling anything he said would only make things worse.

"You know what? I probably should head back to my place." The last thing he wanted was to leave. But he needed to give her time to miss him the way he'd miss her. Time to think about him the way he couldn't stop thinking about her. Time to long for him the way he'd been longing for her since the moment he'd pulled her off the roof and into his arms.

When disappointment flashed in her eyes, it took every ounce of his control not to smile. Especially when she bit her lip and said, "Are you sure? I suppose I could add a little milk to make this go further."

She obviously wanted him to stay, but at the same time, getting too close to him seemed to terrify her.

Why? Who had hurt her? Who had taught her to

be afraid to trust?

Just the thought of anyone hurting Tasha made Daniel's hands fist. He'd never felt this protective of anyone other than his family and the other Mavericks. Certainly not about a woman. Still, she wouldn't miss him, wouldn't long for him, if he stuck around too long today.

"Remember, I'm just down the hill if you need any help with the dogs."

He pressed a kiss to her forehead—a kiss that sent shockwaves through him—and was gone before she could pretend the gentle kiss hadn't sent aftershocks through her too.

Chapter Eight

A storm hit viciously that night, a day earlier than the weatherman predicted. As it raged against the windows, Tasha was afraid the panes would break. The wind ripped the plastic tarp off her roof, the crackle of it flying into the night.

Yet, for all its power, the storm had nothing on the one raging inside her in the aftermath of Daniel's sweet kiss.

The feel of his arms around her in the makeshift kitchen had been powerful enough to make her want to stay there forever, as though she'd finally found a real home after jumping from place to place for so long. Her head on his chest, the spicy man smell of him, the texture of his shirt beneath her fingers, the steady *thump-thump* of his heart in her ear. She'd felt so safe. So warm. Like one of the puppies beneath his gentle hands as he stroked her back.

She'd wanted him to stay for more than soup—so much more—and it had freaked her out. Thankfully, he'd changed his mind about staying for lunch.

God, she was such a bad liar, especially to herself.

She hadn't been *thankful* he'd left. She'd felt bereft. And so were the puppies—she swore they'd been pining for him all afternoon and evening.

Where's the big guy who knows how to scratch us just right? their round eyes seemed to say.

She felt their pain. Daniel not only knew how to rub a puppy's belly, he also knew how to kiss a woman until she was breathless. The mere imprint of his lips on her forehead told her that.

What wouldn't she give to feel his mouth against hers…

She had to remind herself that it wasn't possible. How could a woman with a despicable past—and a desolate future—ever deserve a man like Daniel Spencer?

One of the puppies mewled, and she rushed to the box. The lights had gone out fifteen minutes ago, and she'd lit a hurricane lamp. But she didn't have enough bowls to catch the leaks that were quickly coming down all around them.

"It's okay," she murmured, reaching in to stroke Spanky.

She could only thank God—and Daniel—that they were out of that cave. They would have been soaked, then frozen. They wouldn't have survived the night.

A fat raindrop plopped through the roof onto Darla's head, but it seemed she had no strength to shake it off. Tasha had coaxed the puppies to eat twice more and had given them water, but she feared they still had a ways to go toward full recovery after dehydration and near starvation.

She pulled the crate closer to the wood stove to keep them warm, until another leak appeared and she had to move them again. The bedroom was relatively dry, but the stove's heat hadn't yet penetrated that room.

Boom! A particularly loud crash of thunder shook the house.

Froggy started to howl—even Tasha shrieked in surprise—and when she picked him up to soothe him, Spanky joined in the melee. "It's okay, you guys, I'll keep you safe and warm."

She had two puppies in her arms when her front door flew open, sheets of rain blowing in to soak the floor. Daniel followed the rain in, stepping into her life and her house just when she needed him most.

Again.

★ ★ ★

Free of its ponytail for once, Tasha's hair flowed down her back, black as midnight in the lamplight, silky, shiny. Beautifully touchable as she sat cross-legged with two puppies in her arms.

Daniel shoved the door closed against the wind and rain. "I knocked, but got worried when no one answered. The wind blew the door right out of my hand when I opened it."

She nodded, her hair cascading over her shoulders.

"I couldn't hear anything over the thunder." She bent to kiss a furry head. "But the storm scared the puppies. They keep howling." She glanced into the crate. "Except Darla. Even through the racket, she's barely moved. I'm worried about her." Her fears were written all over her face as she turned from the puppy to him. Her eyes suddenly widened when she took in his drenched-to-the-skin state, his clothing plastered to his chest and thighs. "It couldn't have been safe for you to walk up here. You're soaked."

"I drove the truck." He surveyed his wet clothing and the puddle he was making on the floor. "This was just getting from the driveway to your door."

Not that one more puddle seemed to matter, considering all the bowls and pots and pans that littered the floor of her cabin, the plinking of raindrops a counterpoint to wind and thunder. Rainwater pooled in spots where she'd run out of cookware.

"I noticed your tarps blew off," he said.

The roof had more holes than actual wood. If stars had been out, he'd able to see them right through it. How the heck had she survived the last three wintry months? A beaded raindrop hanging from a beam above chose that moment to drop on her forehead and roll down her nose. He would kill to kiss it off.

"I was going to offer to help you tack them back on," he continued, "but as bad as this storm is becoming, I'm thinking we should head back to my house. My roof is watertight. The fire's going. And there's hot coffee. Good food." In case she was thinking of turning down his offer, he played his trump card. "The cold and damp can't be good for the puppies. Especially Darla. You said she's not doing well." He didn't want to pound home any guilt, but no way was he letting Tasha stay in this falling-down wreck when the next big gust of wind might blow it away. "They need to be somewhere warm and dry. And I've got it."

Right then, Darla made a little snuffling sound from deep in the box. That sealed the deal.

"You're right," Tasha said. "It would be better for the puppies if we went to your place."

Victory. It was so sweet.

Even if he sensed it was only temporary.

★ ★ ★

Daniel went out of his way to be helpful, driving his truck right up to the porch, toting the puppies' box out to it, getting drenched all over again in the process while miraculously keeping the box relatively dry. At his house, he helped her bundle up the puppies, carry in their food, then set them up by his big, lovely fireplace. And he was still working, this time getting dinner ready for them. And later, when she slept in his big bed—which he'd insisted she have because he'd obviously been raised a gentleman—she knew she wouldn't have to be afraid that he'd sneak in while she was sleeping. Daniel wasn't scum like her ex.

No, the only person she had to worry about stepping over the line was herself. She wanted to throw herself into his arms and beg him to make all the bad, all the dark, all the evil go away.

She wanted to lose herself in him and forget everything—and everyone who was hurt because she'd failed to face up to her father's shortcomings.

But Daniel deserved someone better, someone who was able to see the difference between good and bad. Someone brave enough to right all the wrongs, instead of running away.

"Can I do anything to help?" she asked.

"How about cutting up some veggies to grill? I've got red peppers and asparagus."

Thank goodness his outdoor kitchen was covered. The meal he cooked was amazing. Granted, she'd been living on cereal, microwaved soup, baked beans, hot dogs, and scrambled eggs for months. But even if she'd been eating at five-star restaurants every night, Daniel's food would have been delicious, because he'd cooked it and she was eating with *him*.

They sat on the floor on thick cushions, leaning against big beanbags. A fire blazed in the stove insert, and he'd set out lanterns to ward off the dark until the electricity came back on. The puppies lay sleeping in their box, so much more comfortable than they'd been in her cold, wet cabin.

She felt exactly the same way—warm, content, and sated. Even unfinished, this house was more a home than anything she'd ever lived in. It was so Daniel—

big, open, meant for family to come rambling through.

"Where'd you learn to cook like this?" she asked, licking her lips.

"I'm a bachelor," he said with a laugh, though it seemed a tad hoarse as he watched her mouth. "We all know how to barbecue."

"But don't you normally have loads of household staff to do that stuff for you?" There was no point pretending he wasn't a billionaire.

"I have a cook on standby when I don't feel like doing it myself and someone to clean house, but I'm just one person. I don't need a lot." Then he smiled cheekily. "And my mom insisted I learn how to barbecue because my dad always burns the meat."

"I've said this before, but your family sounds won-derful." She was determined to be happy for him without feeling sorry for herself.

"Yeah," he said, though a little frown settled be-tween his eyebrows. With a small shake of his head, he continued, "They're great. You and my sister, Lyssa, would really like each other. She's in Chicago where my parents live. Where we all grew up."

Tasha wanted to know everything about him, even though it was dangerous territory given that the more she knew, the more she liked.

"How did you go from Chicago to all this?" She gestured to his mansion-in-progress.

"I went into contracting right out of high school. College never felt like a great fit for me, and I like to work with my hands. That's why I enjoy building this place. I missed creating something with my own hands. I missed having calluses." Setting his plate on the floor beside him, he held out his palms. "It took a while, but I've got them again."

She remembered his deliciously callused touch from when he'd rescued her, and now she felt the urge to kiss each and every mark on his hands. "What happened next?" Her voice sounded as hoarse as his when he'd laughed a few minutes ago.

"I came up with some new tools, got some patents." He shrugged as though it were a feat anyone might have accomplished. "The money gave me a grub stake. And I moved on from there."

She marveled—who wouldn't? "Your parents must be very proud."

"They're proud of all of us."

He was modest, but she could see how much it meant to him to make his mother and father proud. "You did it for them, didn't you? I get that you wanted to be a success, but all your money, everything you've built, it was so that you could give them everything they didn't have when you were a kid, wasn't it?"

His eyes held hers for a long moment, as though he was stunned by her insight. "Yes, it was. It *is*. I'll never be able to do enough for them. All the Mavericks feel the same way—we wish we could buy them a bigger house, better cars, send them on fancy cruise ships and private jets, give them shopping sprees at the most expensive stores." He shook his head. "But they don't want any of that. All they want is time to spend with us and a house that's big enough to put everyone up for the holidays."

All the things his parents didn't want were exactly the things her father had lied, cheated, and stolen to obtain. And instead of being showered with unconditional love as Daniel had been, Tasha and her brother had merely been pawns in her father's cons. She remembered clearly how he'd trotted them out at business dinners and parties as if to say, *Now that you can see what a great dad I am, you know I must be trustworthy.*

"Tasha? Are you okay?"

She came back to the concern in Daniel's handsome face, the warmth in his deep-brown eyes. "I was just thinking about my family." The words came before she could stop them.

"Did you used to spend a lot of time with them?"

His question was gentle, but far too probing. "We worked together." She shrugged, trying to bury the topic in nonchalance. "But that's all in the past now. And we were talking about you. How did you come by your carpentry skills in the first place?"

They were both well aware that she was pivoting away from talking about herself. The only question was whether Daniel would let her get away with turning the spotlight back on him.

"When we were growing up," he finally said,

"nothing ever got fixed in our tenement unless we did it ourselves. So Dad learned how to mend leaky faucets and running toilets and change the thermostat in the oven and put in new floorboards and Sheetrock."

She was relieved that he'd let her off the hook. Yet there was a part of her that longed to confide in him.

An extremely foolish part that needed to keep its mouth shut.

"He taught you along with the other Mavericks?"

"All five of us definitely know our way around a tool belt. We worked for our keep." Done with his steak, he stretched his legs out in front of him, leaning back against the beanbag, hands behind his head. "We all enjoyed it too."

"There's something really satisfying about completing a job, isn't there?" She much preferred this safe topic of conversation to the *family* minefield. "These past months, I've had more than a few moments when I've been so pleased with the work I'm doing that I just have to stand back and look at it." She'd often felt the same way while building websites, especially when she figured out a new tool or widget. She didn't mention her job, though. It would only trigger more questions.

"Yeah," he agreed. "It's a great feeling. My dad didn't just give us the tools to be able to fix things with our own hands—he showed the other tenants how to fix stuff too." Daniel's expression softened with the tremendous love he felt for his father, for his whole family. "That's where the idea for my DIY show came from. I wanted to emulate Dad by teaching people how to do it themselves and save money. And also to give them an inexpensive place to buy the tools and products they need, aided by helpful assistants to answer their questions. At first, we did demonstrations and classes at the stores, but I wanted to reach as many people as possible, so we transitioned into videos."

It didn't hurt, she thought, that Daniel was so good to look at on the screen, that he smiled often, that his laugh was a deep bass. But he was *so* much better in person. Her reactions to him were more visceral—the curl of desire in her belly, the heat of her skin when he was near.

Just as she'd feared, the more she liked him, the harder it was to keep her distance. Especially in the warm firelight and the candles and lanterns he'd set out to keep the dark at bay, where she felt lulled into wanting what she couldn't have. What she didn't believe she was worthy of. Not anymore.

"Any video requests?" he asked.

"You have to do a video on installing a hot tub," she found herself saying. "I'd love to install one off my bedroom so that I can get into it first thing in the morning, straight out of bed."

"A hot tub? Off your *bedroom*?" His voice sounded strangled, his gaze sizzling hot and riveted on her lips, as though he wanted to devour them. As if he wanted to consume *her*.

The only thing that could have broken the spell

was a puppy whining for food. Otherwise, Tasha might have dived on him and done all the devouring herself.

"I think that's Darla," Tasha said, jumping to her feet and looking into the crate. Sure enough, the little puppy was squawking like a baby bird. "She must be hungry. Which is good, isn't it? It means she's feeling stronger, right?" She was babbling because Daniel's eyes were so intense. As though he could see right through her need to put distance between them. "I'll make some Puppy Chow for her." Spanky grumbled and woke up, closely followed by Froggy. Concentrating on them was better than facing the look in Daniel's eyes, the one that promised to ferret out all her secrets. "We should probably feed the boys too."

"I'll help you." Leaning down to scratch a puppy ear, Daniel was close enough to heat her straight through.

Backing up, she stepped on the edge of her plate, her cutlery rattling to the floor, and she would have tripped if he hadn't grabbed her.

Just as it had when he'd rescued her from the roof, his touch sent hot need racing through her.

"Why don't we let the dogs run around a bit while we make up their food?" Her voice sounded as breathless as she felt.

"Actually," Daniel said, "I should probably take them outside to do some business first."

Talking about the puppies and their potty training should have squashed all sense of desire. Except it didn't. Because watching him pick all three up in his big hands made her whole body hum, turning her wild inside and crazy with need.

He was so gentle. And yet so strong.

So gorgeous.

So sexy.

Get a grip, Tasha.

Only, that was her major problem. She wanted a grip. On him. All over him.

And she was actually spending the night here?

She'd survived falling off the roof. But temptation might very well be the death of her.

Chapter Nine

Daniel breathed in the cold, stormy night air, hoping it would cool him down. Tasha seemed completely unaware of how utterly desirable she was. As far as he could tell, she didn't have a clue what her smiles and laughter did to him.

And she clearly had no idea of the fantasies his mind had conjured up when she'd mentioned hot tubs…

It was going to be a hell of a long night.

By the time he'd returned with the puppies, she'd lined up food bowls on the floor in front of the crate. After he put them down on the hardwood floor, their feet slid out from under them as they tried to scramble to their food.

"Try again, guys." He stood them all up on their paws.

"And girl," Tasha said, kneeling beside him.

Tasha's fresh-rain scent did things to his insides, and he battled an intense desire to nuzzle her hair. Yet there was something so vulnerable about her. He couldn't put his finger on it, but any move he might make felt like he'd be taking advantage of her.

She was nothing like the women he'd dated. Women who knew the score. Who had been around. No one got hurt, and nothing got messy. But Tasha was a whole different toolbox he didn't know his way around.

And he'd be damned if he hurt her.

In the back of his mind, though, he couldn't stop wondering if keeping his distance was more about protecting himself from Tasha. Just as his mother had suggested during their call, maybe that was his MO, the way he'd always held himself back from every other woman, fearing that no relationship could stack up to his parents' perfect, open, honest love story.

Until his mom had started talking about *bumps*.

Damn it, he wasn't letting that thought inside his head right now. Not when he finally had Tasha here for an entire night.

"Sit, Darla." He tapped her behind. "Good girl," he praised. Then he let her eat before doing the same with Spanky.

"Are you trying to train them already?" Tasha gathered up Froggy like a protective mother. "They're just babies."

The affronted frown on her brow made him laugh. "They did their business outside when I told them. So I figure they can learn to sit for a meal. Why don't you try the command?"

She *harrumph*ed, so damn cute the need to kiss her

consumed him all over again. But she set Froggy by a bowl, said, "Sit, Froggy," and tapped his little bottom. When he sat, she applauded him, then let him eat.

"See? It works."

She rolled her eyes at him. "Only if I tap his butt down."

"Good training habits start early."

She narrowed-eyed him this time. "You said you'd never had a pet, so how do you know?"

"Intuition."

"Yeah, right." She laughed.

He loved the way her face lit up when she forgot to be wary. It was just how he wanted her—sweet and hot and laughing.

Without thinking, he reached out to tuck her hair behind her ear. She went still, and his heart beat harder in his chest, throbbing in places way down low. He'd never felt this mixture of desire laced with nerves before.

He'd always asked for what he wanted, never worried about mixed signals, never wondered if someone might get hurt—because none of his previous dates had had any chance of lasting for the long haul. They'd known it as well as he had.

But with Tasha...

His thoughts scattered as she turned to him slightly, her mouth so damn kissable. Trailing his finger around the shell of her ear, he touched her lobe, slid down to her throat, her skin warm to the touch. Her lashes fluttered down, and she finally breathed, her lips parting. Inviting.

He was so close to kissing her. Barely a breath away from drowning in her scent, in her warmth.

"Oh look, see how much Darla's eating all on her own this time." Her voice trembled, but whether it was with desire or nerves, he didn't know. "She's finally on the mend. And so are the other two. They just needed food and water and TLC. Don't you think?"

"I do," he said, squashing his disappointment that she hadn't fallen into his arms. "They're going to be fine."

Maybe he should have kissed her and to hell with thinking things through. But he wanted her to be just as into him as he was into her. He wanted to know he wasn't the only one slowly going crazy with need.

And the truth was that he needed to understand her better before they took that step, so they could avoid any pitfalls waiting around the bend.

When she yawned, it hit him how tired she must be from caretaking the three puppies. Plus, she'd been up way earlier than he had, the realization a potent reminder of how she'd found him naked in his bed this morning. The memory made his voice a little rough around the edges. "It's been a long day, and you've been occupied with these furballs the whole time. It's my turn tonight. Why don't you head up to bed?"

"I like taking care of them," she insisted, "even if

they don't sleep through the night yet." The second big yawn that chased her sentence gave her away.

"Do I need to carry you up there and tuck you in myself?" He'd love it. But it was the baddest of bad ideas considering he didn't trust himself to find the strength to leave.

"No!" The unavoidable sensual undertones of his offer were akin to striking a match beneath her feet. "I'm going." She was already skittering away from him and up the stairs when she called over her shoulder, "Good night."

He sat on the floor with the dogs, stroking them silently until he heard his bedroom door close. "Women." Darla gave him the side-eye, and he brushed a hand over her cute head. "All the ones who ever wanted me, I didn't want. And now that I've found one I can't stop thinking about…"

Darla slipped and slid as she tried to climb into his lap. He picked her up, and she immediately curled into a ball of fluff. Moments later, her brothers were jostling to join her, and before Daniel knew it, he had three warm bodies happily snoring against him.

Family. There was nothing like it to heal you—or, as in the case of the other Mavericks' birth parents, harm you.

He'd learned tonight that Tasha had worked with her family, which was now in the past. But her emotions about it clearly weren't past artifacts, if merely talking about her family could etch that much pain on her face.

Daniel knew from Will, Sebastian, Matt, and Evan's experiences that dealing with bad things from your past wasn't easy. On the contrary, it tended to be a long road, one you could walk only with the people who loved you, people you trusted not to use your pain against you.

Secure in the knowledge that nothing could hurt Tasha while she was in his home, he leaned against the beanbag and closed his eyes, soon joining the puppies in their slumber.

★ ★ ★

Tasha woke to the sun filling Daniel's room. The storm had passed during the night, and the morning was glorious. She stretched luxuriously in his big sleigh bed. Though she should have been more insistent that she didn't need to take his bed, she couldn't deny that the thick, top-quality mattress was an utterly delicious treat after three months on a blow-up bed.

Daniel had said she should use whatever she wanted, and though she didn't like to take advantage of his hospitality, she couldn't resist a shower in his spa-like bathroom.

Nor, on the heels of last night's almost-kiss that had crept into her dreams, could she resist the fantasy of Daniel in there with her, soaping each other…

No, she couldn't think like that. Couldn't allow herself to fall deeper under his spell. Especially now that she'd learned just how difficult his childhood had been—and how hard he'd worked to bring not only himself out of it, but his parents as well.

Daniel deserved to be with a woman just as selfless and good as he was. One who had sound judgment about people, or at the very least, one who hadn't missed every single sign of wrongdoing her entire life. A woman who'd never walked on the wrong side, the way Tasha had with her family.

After showering and towel-drying her hair, she left it hanging loose to air dry. Finally looking at her watch, she shocked herself. It was eleven o'clock. How had she slept that long? It was unheard of.

But she knew exactly why. With Daniel downstairs, she'd felt safe for the first time in months. She hadn't missed the wariness that sometimes crept into his eyes, as though it worried him that he couldn't add up all her pieces into a whole. He was right to be wary, obviously smarter than she by a long shot when it came to not trusting someone completely before you knew enough about them.

At last, she left the bedroom, lured by the scent of freshly brewed coffee. In jeans and a lumberjack shirt, Daniel was all bulging muscles and absolute perfection, freshly showered and his hair still wet. She followed his gaze to the wet footprints on the deck outside and the towel hanging over the rail.

"Did you wash up in the *lake*?" She shivered just imagining it. The water was *cold*.

He ran a hand through his hair, already starting to curl as it dried. "It's a refreshing way to wake up."

His smile threatened to knock her to her knees, as did the image of him jumping naked into the lake. But she needed to be stronger than her hormones and her desires.

In the great room, he'd set plates on the long plank between two sawhorses, normally his workbench but now doubling as a dining table. "Ready for pancakes and eggs?"

"You don't even have a full kitchen in yet," she said. "How can you make pancakes and eggs?"

"You can do anything on a barbecue. It's just another gas flame."

He was too good. Too sweet. Too everything. Weakness stole over her again—the need to stay, the desire to trust him with all her secrets.

But what would he say once he learned that her whole life was a lie? If he knew her family were criminals? And that she'd played a part—no matter how unwitting—in swindling all those people?

She'd already overstayed her welcome, but she couldn't simply hightail it out of here first thing in the morning. Not after he'd been so gracious about letting her stay the night and cooking for her—and not when her furry little charges were snuffling around inside their crate.

She was glad she could mask her emotions for Daniel by training her attention on the puppies. "How are you guys doing this morning?" Kneeling beside them, she reached inside the box to pick up Darla. The little puppy began to lick her fingers. "You're just the sweetest thing."

"I fed them again," Daniel said, "then took them outside to do their business, and they've gotten a couple of catnaps in too. They seem a lot friskier today." He knelt on the floor next to her. "The vet was able to squeeze in their appointment this afternoon before the holiday weekend."

Up here all alone, she sometimes lost track of what day of the week it was. She'd completely forgotten that it was Memorial Day weekend. "Thank you for doing that. You should have woken me. I could have helped."

"I'm glad you got a good night's sleep," he said. "It's been my pleasure, Tasha."

The way he said *pleasure* heated her skin, as if he were whispering delectably naughty things in her ear, especially after referencing her night spent in his bed.

Thankfully, he didn't seem to have a clue about her jumbled emotions as he picked up Spanky and Froggy. "Look what I taught them." Setting both puppies on the floor, he reached into his jeans pocket and brought out a nugget of puppy food. "Sit, Spanky." Before he could tap the puppy's behind, the little guy sat. Froggy did the same, although he did need a tiny reminder with a gentle finger placed on his bottom.

She could hardly believe her eyes, especially when the two puppies got their treats, then began to scamper about, rolling over each other and wrestling.

"They're so smart, and so much better! After just one day." She stroked Darla's head, then put her on the floor. "Did you teach her too?"

Daniel retrieved another bite of kibble from his pocket. But Darla didn't sit. Instead, she began to relieve herself.

"Oh no, you don't." Daniel set her on a thick layer of newspaper Tasha hadn't noticed before. After the puppy was done, she trotted toward her gamboling brothers. "She'll be fine," he told Tasha, looking for all the world like a proud papa. "She just needs to build up her strength." He gestured to one of the folding chairs he'd put by the makeshift table. "And so do you. Eat before everything gets cold."

He'd set out maple syrup and raspberry jam for the pancakes, along with butter, but Tasha placed an egg on top of her pancake and broke the yolk, letting it drizzle down.

"You're even great at making breakfast on a grill," she said after swallowing the first bite.

She was grateful for the delicious food. For his help with the puppies and the feather-soft bed. But all the longing inside her told her it was long past time to get out, so she practically shoveled down the rest of the egg and pancake.

And almost spat it out when the front door shook with a loud banging.

"Who the heck is that?" Daniel said.

Tasha sat frozen as he rose to answer it. Oh God, had the investigators changed their minds? Had they decided she was as bad as her father? They'd surely send her to prison, where she would rot for being so weak, for never questioning her family, for always seeing only the good in them, and for being stupid enough to succumb to Eric's lying charms.

But the four men barreling through Daniel's front door weren't wearing uniforms or dark suits. Instead, they were dressed in jeans, T-shirts, and flannel.

And each of them was as gorgeous as Daniel. Well, *nearly* as gorgeous.

"What are you guys doing here?" Daniel asked as he exchanged friendly backslaps and manly hugs.

Tasha's heart was still jumping in her chest, though it was obvious these were his friends.

"We couldn't let you spend the holiday weekend all alone," said a member of the handsome bunch, this one with hair so dark it was almost black.

That was when another of Daniel's friends spotted her. Pushing up his sunglasses, he smiled. "Looks like you're not alone, after all."

Her fear vanished, replaced by embarrassment. Here she was having breakfast with Daniel, her feet still bare, as if she'd been here all night. Which she had been, but—

What would they think?

But she already knew—they'd assume she was their friend's secret mountain lover. From everything she'd heard, they'd be protective of Daniel, ready to swoop in to save him from a gold digger.

"This is Tasha," Daniel told them. "She lives up the hill, and her roof sprang a few leaks last night in the storm." He winked at her, obviously trying to put her at ease. "More than a few, actually."

She rose and said hello as Daniel made the introductions. Will Franconi was the dark-haired one who'd explained their arrival, and Matt Tremont had first spied her at the sawhorse table. Sebastian Montgomery had devil-dark good looks. Evan Collins, wearing slacks and a polo shirt, was the last to shake her hand.

They were all tall and fit and vibrant, filling the house with so much more than just their size. They each shook her hand firmly, but she was certain they must be wondering what a scraggly woman like her was doing with the magnificent Daniel Spencer, if not trying to con him out of his money?

Lord knew she had plenty of experience with that. *Con* was her family's middle name, after all.

Spanky barreled across the living room, Froggy hot on his trail, both of them knocking into Matt's legs. He went down on his haunches.

"Who the heck are these guys?" he asked as Spanky launched himself at Matt's shoelaces and began a tug of war.

Over the past few days, Tasha had gathered from the details Daniel revealed that his Maverick friends were also billionaires. Daniel might be a really nice anomaly who didn't mind puppies weeing on his floor and tearing at his shoelaces, but surely other billionaires wouldn't be so easygoing.

She was just about to pick up Spanky when Matt surprised her by laughing as he helped the puppy bite another piece of his shoelace.

"Tasha found them in the woods," Daniel explained. "They'd been abandoned."

She grabbed at the chance to justify her presence in Daniel's house. "They were hiding in an old rabbit warren, and I heard them crying when I was hiking. Daniel helped me get them out. The poor little things were starving." She retrieved Darla, who'd been watching cautiously from her position close to the box, and held the little girl close. Both of them, it seemed, needed reassurance. "We've been feeding them every couple of hours, and they've got a date with the vet this afternoon to make sure everything's okay. Daniel's already been up and down the houses on the road to see if anyone knows anything about them. But no one does."

Too late, she realized she was rambling like a wild woman. Thankfully, Froggy was causing a bit of a commotion as he decided Spanky had the right idea and went for Evan's shoelaces, tugging and growling playfully.

"That's Froggy," Daniel told them. "The big one is Spanky." He pointed at the bundle of fluff in Tasha's hands. "And this is Darla."

Sebastian laughed. "The Little Rascals. Interesting choice in names."

"Daniel wanted to call them Larry, Curly, and Moe," Tasha said, raising an eyebrow in Daniel's direction. "Or Groucho, Harpo, and Chico."

"I'm pretty sure," Daniel reminded her with a grin, "that you suggested the Marx Brothers, not me."

Tasha belatedly realized his friends had fallen silent, watching them banter. Especially Evan, whose eyes narrowed as he gazed at her.

Why couldn't she remember to hold her cards close to her chest?

Froggy began to piddle on the floor and commanded their attention as Daniel scooped the puppy up and got him to the newspapers. "Obviously," Daniel said, "they're still in training."

"Noah will go crazy when he sees them." Matt, still crouching, twirled Spanky around in circles until the puppy started to chase his own tail. "A puppy is every six-year-old's dream."

When Froggy ran back into the melee, Tasha set Darla on the floor. She'd never seen big, powerful, successful men go all gooey like this. Especially when Daniel showed off the trick he'd taught the puppies, even if it was only to sit when their rump was patted.

Her ex, by contrast, had always acted like he was too cool, too important, to moon over babies or puppies or kittens. It was, she realized now, a crucial test of whether a man was worthy or not.

Sebastian got Darla to sit for a piece of kibble. Soon, the puppies were running amok again, snatching at shoelaces, tumbling all over the floor, and skidding into the sawhorses. The men were just as bad—big, jovial kids.

Tasha was utterly charmed.

She wanted to stay, wanted to get down on her knees and play too, wanted to learn all about them— ask them what they did, whether they were married, how many kids they had. But at the same time, seeing them together made her miss her friends so much that her heart ached.

Weakness hit her all over again. Along with the sure knowledge that she didn't belong here, no matter how much she wished she did.

Chapter Ten

"It's been great to meet all of you," Tasha said, "but I need to get back to my place and see if it's still standing after the storm."

Daniel had been aware of her the whole time that she'd stood back, simply watching. Her avid gaze betrayed how badly she wanted to dive in and play, but when it appeared she might lose herself in the fun, she seemed determined to force herself to back off.

He'd had her to himself all last night, and that had to be enough for now. The more he pushed, the more she'd shy away. Then he'd never get the answers he was looking for, the ones he hoped would put his mind at ease when it came to considering a full-fledged relationship with her.

Unfortunately, patience had never been his strong suit. He'd always gotten in there with his hands and tools to fix whatever was broken or to build whatever he needed. But he couldn't simply mold Tasha into what he wanted her to be. She was fiercely independent and more than capable of fixing things for herself.

"Okay, guys," he made himself say. "Let's get the

puppies into the box so Tasha can carry them home."

"Harper sent a picnic basket for the drive up," Will said. "I'll clean it out, and we can use that."

But once they'd emptied the basket, the puppies had other ideas for the perfect game. Just when one puppy was settled in, another would jump out. Even Darla found the energy to join in the fun.

They were all hysterical with laughter by the time the puppies were firmly tucked into the basket with a towel and Tasha had it hooked over her elbow, the bag of Puppy Chow under her other arm as she backed toward the door.

"Don't forget the vet appointment," Daniel reminded her at the door. "Three o'clock. I'll bring the crate up when I come to get you."

The guys were on him the minute she closed the door, demanding to know all about her.

Daniel tried to play it down for Tasha's sake. She wouldn't appreciate his friends making something out of her being at his breakfast table. "She's my neighbor. I let her borrow some tools and helped her out with the puppies, and when her roof was leaking last night, it made sense for them to come here." Evan didn't look convinced, but before he could say anything, Daniel asked, "So how did your better halves all agree to let you go on a holiday weekend?"

Will pulled over a beanbag and plopped into it, eyebrows raised. "You suck at changing the subject. Especially since we're not going to leave you alone until you tell us what we want to know."

Daniel stopped fighting the inevitable. These were his best friends in all the world. They'd been through hell and back together. They'd each gotten out too, just the way they'd sworn they would, every one of them hitting the big time without forgetting their past or how much Susan and Bob had helped them. When the money started rolling in, the first thing the Mavericks had done was buy his mom and dad a new house in a decent neighborhood. Daniel hadn't needed to ask any of them to pitch in and help; that came naturally. And, of course, when they each found the woman of their dreams, he'd cheered for them.

He pulled up one of the folding chairs and sat. "Here's what I know so far: Tasha has been living in that run-down shack for three months, almost completely unplugged from the world. She's not afraid of hard work—you should see what she's done to her cabin so far, even installing the toilet completely by herself, just from watching do-it-yourself videos."

"We should have known you'd fall for a woman who gets breathless over your tool belt," Sebastian said on a laugh.

Daniel laughed too, but didn't say aloud that *her* tool belt actually made *him* hot. "She's putty in those puppies' paws and would have done absolutely anything to save them. And..." He looked at his best friends, knowing they'd understand better than anyone, even if it was something he was still trying to wrap his own head around. "She makes me feel something." He knocked his fist into his chest. "Here."

"Finally," Sebastian said. "We've been wondering when you were going to meet someone worthy of you." Matt and Will grinned and nodded their agreement.

Only Evan held out, asking, "But is she really what you need?"

"Hell, yes," Daniel said, immediately defensive on her behalf. Though he still hadn't learned nearly enough about her, he realized that he'd already discovered everything that counted.

She was sweet and strong and caring and determined.

On top of it all, she made his heart race and his palms sweat—and every cell in his body *crave*.

"I want to believe you," Evan said, "but what do you really know about her?" He looked at the empty puppy box. "Apart from how much she likes dogs and how great she is at installing toilets. Sounds to me like she's hiding out from something."

"Don't listen to anything that guy says." Sebastian jerked a thumb at Evan. "He's still gun-shy after Whitney. Always looking for the catch."

"Paige should have broken you of that habit by now," Will said to Evan. "You've got a good woman, so you can start looking on the bright side."

"I know exactly how good I've got it," Evan agreed. "But I'm still going to keep looking out for my friends."

Of them all, Evan had experienced the very worst where relationships were concerned. With Matt a close second. Thankfully, they'd both finally found incredible women they loved and who loved them back with equal fervor.

Will chimed in with his vote of confidence. "I'll bet Mom will love Tasha." Susan Spencer's approval was everyone's litmus test. "Can you believe it's been a year since our last Memorial Day barbecue?"

A year since Will had brought Harper and her brother, Jeremy, into their group, and six months since they'd married. Memorial Day had been the beginning of the truly big changes in their lives. Daniel suspected it had also been the day Evan started to see his now ex-wife, Whitney, for what she truly was, after she'd gone ballistic when Jeremy spilled a margarita on her. Susan, of course, had been instrumental in the positive changes for her sons.

Daniel was tempted to ask his foster brothers if his mother had said anything to any of them about *bumps*. But he knew they saw his parents' marriage exactly as he did—as the one truly perfect, honest relationship out there, with total commitment, never doubting each other. And he didn't want to darken that perfection for any of the guys. Especially if his mom hadn't actually meant anything by her strange comment.

"It's been a good year," Daniel finally said. "But where's Jeremy? Why didn't you bring him along?"

"He's going to camp." Will put his hands behind his head and scooched deeper into the beanbag. "He's been dying to go, and it starts tomorrow. Otherwise, he'd have loved to come with us."

Jeremy was eighteen, but he'd had a bicycle accident when he was a kid—hit by a car—and now had the cognitive ability of a seven-year-old. He was a great person, and he adored Will like an older brother. Will felt exactly the same about him.

"Ari's got a ton of fun things planned for Noah while we're gone." Like a man totally besotted, Matt smiled from his spot on one of the beanbags. "Mommy and son time. She couldn't wait to have Noah all to herself." Ari would soon be Noah's stepmom, and the little guy loved her like a mother.

"Bro-cation, here we come," Sebastian said.

Daniel wasn't fooled. "Charlie kicked you out so she could have some peace and quiet to finish her latest masterpiece, didn't she?"

Charlie was a fantastic artist, her medium being metal, and had created the work of art adorning the center lobby of Sebastian's San Francisco headquarters. She'd also helped Sebastian appreciate his own artistic talents.

Sebastian confessed, "She did suggest that a few days with the guys would get me the hell out of her hair."

Their laughter rang through the open rafters.

Daniel was glad his friends had come. Once Tasha

saw the kind of men he called brothers—good, solid friends who would do anything for each other—maybe then she would let down her guard and trust him.

Of course, that meant he'd have to devise ways to spend time with her this weekend. Fortunately, their visit to the vet was only hours away.

* * *

Tasha had always wondered what it would be like to be part of a big family, to have a real home you could run to when things were bad. Now, after traveling to the vet with Daniel and his friends—who scooped up nearly every squeaking, squishing, rattling, and tug-of-war toy in the pet store—she was pretty sure she knew.

Daniel's family was wonderfully fun, crazy, and out of control in all the best ways.

Only Evan stood back a bit. All afternoon, she'd felt his eyes on her, as though he was assessing her. Taking in everything she said, breaking it down, then splicing the pieces back together, as if that might help him figure out what she was hiding.

It was utterly unnerving. Not only because she knew damn well just how much she had to hide. But also because she couldn't seem to stop her headlong fall for Daniel...and wishing that things could be different.

He had been so wonderful at the vet, asking all the right questions: What should they feed the puppies, did they need extra vitamins, when should they have their shots, suggestions on training. The vet gave the puppies clean bills of health, saying they'd been rescued before permanent damage was caused by dehydration or starvation. In the vet's expert opinion, the puppies were a German shepherd mix and about five weeks old, so too young for some of the shots they'd need. They'd have to come back, which meant more time Tasha would get to spend with Daniel.

Unless Evan figured things out first.

"Hey," Daniel said softly, pulling her slightly away from the group in the pet store aisle. "This stuff is on me, okay? My friends are going crazy, so I'm paying for it."

He must have seen the worried look in her eyes and assumed it was because she didn't have the money for dog toys. "I don't—"

He put a finger to her lips, and a sizzling hot flame burst to life inside her. Her whole heart and soul ached to lean into his touch and ask for more. But she couldn't.

"I'm paying," he said again. "For the vet, for the toys, the crate, for everything. No argument."

"But—"

He moved in on her, so close she was hypnotized by his delicious all-male scent. She could close her eyes in a room and pick him out immediately.

"No buts." His eyes were such a deep, alluring coffee color. She wanted to fall into his gaze. Into his arms.

It was a seduction, like the prelude to a kiss. Every nerve in her body shouted to feel his mouth on hers.

Until, over Daniel's shoulder, Evan's assessing gaze hit her like an avalanche.

"Thank you," she said, trying to act normally, as though she wasn't burning up from the inside out from that one simple touch. Feeling awkward and worried about what Evan—and the rest of the Mavericks—must think of her drooling all over their friend, she said, "I appreciate everything you're doing."

As Daniel frowned at her polite response, she was sure he was going to call her on it.

Fortunately, Will drew everyone's attention as he scooped up Froggy and asked, "What about homes for them? My brother-in-law, Jeremy, would be ecstatic to have this little guy."

"And my son, Noah, would love this dude." Matt stroked Spanky's ruff. "Maybe as a late birthday present."

When Sebastian reached for Darla, her heart wrenched extra hard at the thought of letting her go.

"Tasha definitely needs to keep one." Daniel leaned in close, saying for her alone, "To replace the cat you had to leave behind when you were a kid."

He'd recalled her offhand comment. How could a man be so thoughtful, remembering details, big and little? Then come up with a way to make things better?

"What about you?" she asked. Something flashed in his eyes, a longing that was gone so quickly she thought she'd read it wrong. "Don't you want one of the puppies?"

"I travel too much." He turned to his friends. "Let's think about it, guys. It's a great idea to give them all good homes, but we should keep them together until they've had all their shots."

"Noah will be begging to visit," Matt warned.

"And Jeremy will be driving Harper crazy asking when, when, when." The smile on Will's face shone with love. Jeremy might be his brother by marriage, but Tasha saw vividly that he owned a huge piece of the big man's heart.

Though she hated to let any of the dogs go, she felt the rightness of giving them to families who would love them with all their hearts. She touched Daniel's arm. "I really can't keep three dogs." She lowered her voice. "I'm not sure I should keep even one."

"You have to keep Darla," Daniel insisted. "She needs you."

Tasha was suddenly close to tears. Maybe it was all the changes over the last few months. The loneliness and despair. Followed by the warmth and cuddliness of the puppies. Then the Mavericks with their laughter and antics.

And most of all, Daniel, bringing such unexpected joy and desire into her life.

It was almost as if she'd finally come home.

Chapter Eleven

The men dropped off Tasha and the puppies at her place, carrying in the new crate, the dog toys, and all the other gear they'd bought. Once inside, they marveled at what she'd accomplished on her own, and Daniel loved seeing her bask in the glow of their compliments. Unfortunately, she turned down their offer to join them at his place for drinks and a barbecue dinner, insisting they'd come to have a guys' weekend and she'd only cramp their style.

"I still can't believe Tasha did all of that by herself," Will said as the five of them sat on the back deck drinking beer. "And from watching *your* DIY videos, no less." His grin took away any heat Daniel might have otherwise felt from the dig.

"But that roof—it's still a total mess." Sebastian shook his head. "I'm surprised she was willing to buy a place like that."

"We can't let her do it alone." Matt clearly couldn't believe Daniel wasn't fixing her roof right this minute.

"She's extremely independent," Daniel said. "The only reason she's accepted my help at all so far is because of the puppies." He would have done so much more for her if he didn't believe his actions would chase her off.

"She can't refuse *all* of us," Will insisted.

"But why the need to be so self-sufficient?" Evan mused. "Seems to me that she doesn't want anyone getting too close. And I can't stop wondering about the reasons."

Sebastian immediately overrode him. "The *why* of it doesn't matter. I've only known her a day and I'm already certain she's a great person. Everyone has their issues, their demons, and we all deal with them in our own ways. The five of us know that better than anyone."

"We sure as hell do," Will agreed. "But regardless of whether she's dealing with demons or not, one thing is certain—it's going to take more than some videos and determination to fix that roof anytime soon." He smiled broadly. "Good thing she's got a handy group of guys hanging out nearby."

"We could have it done by the end of the weekend." Matt agreed.

They weren't saying anything Daniel hadn't already thought. But they didn't know Tasha like he did. "You guys really aren't getting just how badly she wants to take care of herself."

"And *you* really aren't getting just how badly we want to help her," Will said.

"Besides," Sebastian added, "Mom would read you

the riot act for not helping someone in dire need."

"Mom understands independence."

"She sure does." Will whipped out his phone and pushed speed dial. "But that won't stop her from agreeing that we should put a new roof on Tasha's cabin tomorrow."

Even as Will held the phone to his ear, Daniel had the glimmer of a plan. The guys might be right. Tasha wouldn't feel like it was *him* pressuring her if they *all* offered to help. And hopefully, she wouldn't feel there were strings attached either. If you couldn't accomplish a task one way, he'd always thought, you found another. And this way just might work.

"Mom, what are you up to tonight?" Will winced at her response. "You're watching *John Wick: Chapter 2*? That is a seriously violent movie." He rolled his eyes at her retort. "I'll let you get back to the mayhem in a few minutes, but right this second, Daniel needs your encouragement to help his neighbor fix her leaky roof." He nodded. "Yes, we've all met her and she's great." Grinning at Daniel, he added, "Really great." He laughed at something Susan said. "I'm handing the phone over right now. Love you. Give a big hug to Dad." Then he shoved the phone at Daniel while the others snickered.

"He's in for it now," Sebastian said in a gleeful tone.

"I've been waiting for an update on your neighbor," Daniel's mother said when he took the phone, scowling at the others. "Good thing Will decided to call."

Daniel would have called earlier, but he'd still been chewing on her remark about bumpy relationships—and the ring of personal experience in her words. Standing, he wandered back into the house, away from the others.

"Were you ever serious with anyone before Dad?"

"No. Your father is the only man I've ever loved."

So much for hoping she'd been talking about someone else. He waited for her to question why he was asking, but she didn't. It was, honestly, kind of weird how silent she'd gone.

"So," he said into the empty space, "it's been a busy couple of days up here in the mountains." He told his mother about Tasha finding Darla, Spanky, and Froggy in the cave, how together they'd hand-fed them every few hours through the first day and night, then outfitted them with a new crate and chew toys galore.

"Tasha sounds so sweet and caring."

"She is, Mom. Fixing up her cabin, helping the puppies, the work she used to do as a graphic designer—all of those things light her up and make her happy."

"She sounds amazing, Daniel. The boys seem to love her. She's wonderful with puppies. And she loves your videos. If you ask me, you should snap her up right now. And of course you and the boys should fix her roof."

Despite his mom's edict, he ran a hand through his hair, thinking of his earlier concerns. Questions that had been echoed by Evan, although in a much harsher form. "I agree, we should definitely help with her roof. We'll start tomorrow, even if we have to think on our feet to convince her." He'd made up his mind on that before he even took the phone from Will. "But what bothers me is that I still haven't figured out what drove her to give up her career and come here to live in a run-down dump in the woods. And why she's so intent on going it alone."

"I'm sure she has her reasons for wanting to be left alone and to keep herself closed off to everyone," his mother said, echoing Sebastian's thoughts. "Very good reasons, I'm guessing."

Though his mother was talking about Tasha, Daniel couldn't help but wonder if she was also referring to herself—as if she'd once been in a similar sticky position where she'd thought she needed to hide out, away from everyone she cared about and who cared about her.

It was that weird note of personal experience in her tone that made him antsy.

"But maybe," his mother continued, "what she really needs is the right person to come along and show her that it's safe to open herself back up. Someone who isn't going to run when she gets scared and tries to push him away, even if it's the last thing she really wants to do." She paused for a moment. "Take it from me, I know all about it."

Daniel's heart pounded loudly, pulsing in his ears. Was she going to divulge something about her relationship with his father that he'd never known?

"How do you know?" The words croaked from his throat.

"Will was so tough. Matt was so desperate to show he didn't need us. Sebastian wanted to hide his artistic talent for fear of ridicule. And Evan couldn't admit how badly he needed a mother. None of my boys were anywhere near ready to open up when they first came to live with us. Your father and I had to be so persistent, even if it sometimes felt like our love was driving them away, rather than bringing them closer."

But what about Dad? Did something happen between the two of you?

Though the questions were on the tip of his tongue, they never made it all the way out. Not only because he was nervous about hearing her response, but also because something told him his mother wasn't ready to completely confide in him.

And if there *was* anything to confide, was it his business to dredge it up all these years later? Especially if it changed everything he'd believed to be true for so long...

"What if I *think* I'm helping," he finally said, "but really I'm only mucking things up more for her?"

"You might make things worse." His mom was always cheerful, but never sugarcoated. "Or maybe that's just the excuse you're giving yourself, the worry you're clinging to, so that you don't have to risk putting your heart out there for her."

He'd taken risks in a dozen different ways—he'd put his money on the line, gambling with his patents, hoping he could actually sell the products, risking the whole operation by going global, overextending his resources. Even the DIY show had been a gamble. He thought of the moment Tasha had paused the video on that first day, leaving his mouth gaping. That was all people might have seen, just a gaping mouth. It had been wild speculation.

But the truth was that in all his risk-taking, his heart had never been up for grabs.

"What's really holding you back, Daniel?"

He wanted to ask her the same thing. Instead, he answered the question about Tasha. "I'm just wary because she's wary. I can't help feeling she's hiding something."

"Maybe she is. When you're young, you don't always make the right decisions. You get yourself all mixed up. You're not even sure what's right or wrong anymore. You do what your family thinks you should do."

"*Your* family?" He stressed that one word. His grandparents had been gone by the time he was a toddler. He'd never known them. And oddly, now that he thought about it, his mom never talked about them.

He could hear her breathing, as though she'd been

running. Or was panicking about something. "I meant Tasha's family. I'm just being hypothetical. You know what I mean. You just..." She trailed off into nothingness.

But he no longer believed that she was being hypothetical. Or was simply talking about Tasha.

"Mom—"

"I have to go now, Daniel."

"But, Mom—"

"I said I have to go." If he wasn't mistaken, she'd actually snapped at him. His mother, who *never* snapped, who always had words of wisdom, who always knew exactly what to say. Then she did the weirdest thing of all. "I'll talk to you later." She didn't even say his dad was calling her back to watch the movie. She was simply gone.

Daniel stared at his phone, half expecting the line to still be open, that she was coming right back. But his screen went blank.

This was more than mere *bumps*. His mother had fumbled and over-explained. Then she'd hung up on him.

Something had happened in his parents' marriage, he was nearly certain.

And he was very much afraid that whatever it was would bring into question all his beliefs about the very foundation of what marriage and love were supposed to be.

Chapter Twelve

Tasha had taken only one sip of her morning coffee when the pounding of work boots pummeled her porch and male voices boomed in the air. She opened the door to five big men with impressive tool belts and was instantly overpowered by their size, their good looks, their innate confidence—as if they owned the world.

Which, among them all, they practically did.

Daniel stood in front like their emissary, too beautiful for words. "We're here to help. Especially with the roof. But anything else you want done too."

Her mouth opened, and the only thing that came out was a stunned, "The five of you came to help me?"

Tears of gratitude pricked at her eyes that these powerful, successful men—four of whom were, for all intents and purposes, strangers—would offer to help rebuild her cabin.

These past months, she'd been so focused on how she could have missed the darkness inside her family that it was hard to wrap her head around such a selfless offer. One she badly needed, considering her cabin truly had been uninhabitable during the recent storm. There was no way she and the puppies could make it through another one.

"Working vacation," Matt said, his smile as wide as his face. His son must be absolutely lovable.

"We all spend too much time at our desks," Sebastian added, "and need a good workout."

"Speak for yourself." Will flexed his biceps. "I get plenty of workout time."

They amazed her with their humor, always ribbing each other. Five big, happy, smiling guys...who surely would abhor her if they knew her story. Especially given that she couldn't accept their help, then immediately shove them out the door again. They'd want to get to know her. Good God, what if they wanted her to meet their wives and girlfriends?

She couldn't do it. As desperate as she was to mix with people again, to talk and laugh, she couldn't allow it.

As if he could read everything written on her face, Daniel said softly, "It's okay, Tasha. We want to do this. It's fun for us. There's no obligation."

She wanted it too—wanted the camaraderie and the conversation and the fun more than she'd ever wanted anything in her life. Well, apart from Daniel's kiss. She wanted that more than her next heartbeat.

But the only right thing to do was turn them down. It wasn't penance otherwise, was it?

"It's really sweet of you all," she said, "but I haven't

ordered the materials I need. So there's nothing to be done yet."

Will slapped Daniel on the back. "We've got a home-improvement mogul in our midst, remember?"

Sebastian hooked his thumb over his shoulder. "And a Top Notch store just over the hill in Carson City with a warehouse chock full of anything you could possibly need."

"Even better," Matt put in, "you can get it at cost."

She looked at Daniel, and he spread his hands in a don't-blame-me-that-they're-dying-to-help gesture.

They had her beaten all around. Even Evan, though he hadn't uttered a single cajoling comment, wore his tool belt. They were clearly determined to pitch in. En masse, they would charm the heck out of any person they'd ever met.

But hadn't falling for *charming* already gotten her into enough trouble? Then again, if she'd known any of the Mavericks before meeting Eric, she surely would have seen right through him. His versions of *charming* and *powerful* were paper-thin by comparison.

She was still fighting with herself when one of the puppies started to whine in the crate, whimpering for her to let their hunky new friends inside.

"How is Noah's little Spanky?" Matt's eyes danced.

"He's great. And always hungry."

Will stepped into the action too. "I told Jeremy about his new puppy before he left for camp this morning. He was so happy that Harper didn't even get upset at my highhandedness. Plus, I'm pretty sure she's been secretly hoping for a dog."

How could Tasha resist them? And how could she resist Daniel when he looked at her like that—as though her happiness was directly responsible for his?

At last, she held the door wide and stepped to the side. "Come on in."

Giving her a huge smile, Sebastian retrieved a measuring tape from his voluminous tool belt and got straight to work with Will, Evan, and Matt.

Meanwhile, Daniel surprised her by grabbing her coat, taking her hand, and drawing her outside, his warmth and strength momentarily—and deliciously—engulfing her. The sun sparkled on the lake below them, dazzlingly beautiful, and Daniel had to let her go as the trail narrowed. She missed his touch more than she wanted to admit.

"What are they measuring?" she asked, stopping at a rock outcropping to view her cabin.

"Floors, walls, kitchen. They'll do the roof too. You can use the measurements whenever you're ready. We'll add them to that app I showed you, if you'd like."

"Daniel, I—"

He put his finger to her lips. It drove her crazy when he did that, making every cell in her body tremble for a taste of him.

"I promise I'm not going to steamroll you. I just want to help." He smiled his killer smile. "And my mom ordered us to be gentlemanly and help you out."

"You talked to your mother about me?"

"Of course I did."

She was stunned by this news, but tried not to show it as she said, "So you're doing this because your mother told you to?" She imagined a tiny white-haired lady shaking her rolling pin at her five able-bodied sons. Of course they'd do anything she ordered.

He tucked away a lock of hair that had escaped her ball cap. Her body tingled with awareness at the light touch.

"Well, I'm definitely *not* doing this because you're having a *Bad Hair Day*." He tapped her cap, and she laughed as she remembered the slogan stitched on this one. "Your hair is beautiful."

"Thank you," she said, "but I swear I wasn't looking for compliments when I put it on."

"I'm not complimenting. I'm just stating a fact." He ran the length of her ponytail slowly through his fingers, and she shivered as though he were touching so much more—her lips, her cheeks, her body. "And I'm doing this because I want to." His voice was as gentle as his touch. "I hate the thought of you being in a house that leaks. You don't even have a working stove or a real bed. But my friends and I have the means and the skills to help. And Sebastian's right—I have a warehouse full of everything you need."

"I'm grateful, I really am." But that's not how she sounded. All because she couldn't tell him that she was scared—or why. She especially couldn't explain why she didn't deserve all the wonderful things he and his friends wanted to do for her.

"Just take one minute." He seduced her with his deep voice, his expressive gaze. "Close your eyes." He lightly touched her lids.

With his voice and scent surrounding her, making her knees so weak she had to reach out and hold on to him with one hand, she had no choice but to do what he said.

"Now tip your head back and imagine."

"Imagine what?" she whispered, though she was already visualizing being in his soft bed, with his big hands on her, his muscled body over hers.

"Your cabin. The way you want it to be."

In her mind's eye, all she could see was her future hot tub. And the two of them in it together. Naked and wet.

"Tell me what you want."

I want you to touch me.

"I see log cabin walls."

"What else do you see?"

You above me. I can taste your naked skin.

"Hardwood floors. With a slate hearth for the wood stove."

"Tell me more," he said, his deep voice as enticing as all the small touches he constantly showered on her.

"There's a counter separating the main room from the kitchen, with barstools, so I don't need a kitchen table."

"That's perfect," he murmured as if he were talking about the feel of her skin against his.

"Maple kitchen cabinets. Maple floors. It's light and open and airy."

"Good." He paused and lowered his voice to an even deeper tone. "Now tell me about the bedroom."

She shivered as she sank further into her fantasy of the two of them tangled up together, his body heat surrounding her.

"French doors leading out to a small deck."

"And the hot tub."

She bit her lip. "Of course." She saw him in the bubbling water, reaching for her.

"Do you want it?"

"*Yes.*" God, yes. What she wouldn't give to finally have a home, to finally have a place—and a man—she wouldn't have to leave behind the way she'd had to for so many years.

She opened her eyes because she couldn't bear the fantasies anymore. He was close enough for her to make out the dark cocoa laced with milk chocolate in his eyes.

"You can have it, Tasha. Let me help your dreams come true."

This wasn't what her time here in the forest, on this mountain, was supposed to be about. She wasn't supposed to build her own dreams after playing a part in helping her father and brother crush those of so many other people. Yet here she was, on the verge of letting Daniel help her.

Then it hit her—he'd be leaving soon. She'd be alone again.

And nothing would hurt more than watching him go.

Maybe *that* was the reason she'd been compelled to come to Tahoe, to buy this cabin. Because she was destined to meet Daniel, to fall for him, to want him, to need him. To *love* him.

And then to lose him.

It would, she knew with perfect certainty, be the ultimate atonement for her mistakes.

The lump in her throat was so big she could barely speak around it. "Okay, Daniel, you've convinced me." It was nearly impossible to keep the tears from falling as she said, "Make my dreams come true."

Chapter Thirteen

Daniel took Tasha to his store in Carson City and helped her pick out slate for the hearth, log cabin paneling for the walls, and hardwood for the floors. They chose roofing material and new leafless gutters based on the guys' measurements and decking for the sagging porch. They wandered the kitchen displays, checking out cabinets and countertops, appliances and fittings. Everything she purchased, he got for her at cost.

He wanted to give her so much more.

The least he could do was buy her a ball cap that read, *Carpenters know how to nail it.*

She put it on right there in the store, and he nearly threw the rest of his caution to the wind and kissed her. All day, he'd been overwhelmed by the heat of her skin, the scent of her. Not to mention their earlier talk, which seemed to be about so much more than simply planning her house.

Could she possibly know how much he wanted to make all her dreams come true?

With her eyes closed, her body so close, so touchable, kissing her had been a temptation that was almost his undoing. And it sure as hell didn't help matters that the phrase on the ball cap gave him *seriously* hot fantasies.

The roofing materials were all he could fit in the truck bed, and the rest would be delivered tomorrow. Shortly after they returned to the cabin, the guys got to work, and the woods rang with the sound of hammers and nail guns. As long as everything went according to plan, her roof would be done tomorrow.

He hadn't forgotten a present for the puppies, having picked up chicken wire to build a simple outside enclosure. Soon, the dogs were in the pen, wrestling in the fresh air.

Daniel stood behind Tasha as she watched through the window. "They're getting better every day." Her voice was a sigh of relief.

"More like every hour. It's amazing." The little creatures were incredibly resilient.

"Thank you for today," she said softly, though she was still looking out the window. "With your wholesale prices, I didn't have to spend anywhere near as much as I thought I would."

He breathed in her sweet shampoo scent, aching to put his hands on her shoulders and pull her against him. "You're welcome." He wanted to say so much more, but he was trying to be patient, telling himself to take things one step at a time. First, he'd make her dreams for her cabin come true. Then he'd convince her that *he* should be part of those dreams too.

Despite his ongoing misgivings about the *bumps* his mother might be hiding, she was right when it came to taking a risk—he hadn't pushed Tasha, but he also hadn't pushed himself. If he didn't risk his heart now, he would never know if what he and Tasha might have together would be worth everything he had to give. And he'd never know whether he'd discovered the woman and the love he'd always been hoping for.

Not if he didn't put his heart out there completely, perfect or not.

To do that, he had to spend more time with Tasha, draw her out, and ultimately get her to trust him. Part of him burned to tell her about his mom's strange words, as if disclosing his confusion and his feelings would help Tasha reveal herself to him. But right now, he sensed she had too many of her own worries for him to do that.

He hadn't even laid his concerns on the Mavericks. He didn't have all the facts, and freaking them out over something that might be nothing...no way, he couldn't do it. Besides, was it even his business to talk about his mother's stuff behind her back? He didn't have a really good answer, so for now, it would remain his issue to think through without burdening everyone else.

Moving away from the window, Tasha said, "I should get started on the kitchen plan."

It gave him a reason to push his dilemma to the background again. "I'll show you how to use the app."

"You don't need t—" She stopped herself. "I mean, thank you. That would be great."

"Like I said before, you don't need to thank me for anything. I'm enjoying myself. And don't forget, there'll be hell to pay if my mom thinks the five of us haven't given your cabin everything we've got." It was an exaggeration, but it had worked before to help Tasha get over her hesitancy. He didn't feel guilty about using it again.

"I keep forgetting about your little white-haired mom shaking her rolling pin at five strapping young men and ordering them to help out the neighbor."

"*Little white-haired mom?*" He laughed so hard he nearly cried. "Mom will go into hysterics when she hears that."

"Oh no," Tasha said, her cheeks turning pink. "I didn't mean to offend her or you."

"My mom is impossible to offend. She'd have to be, after raising the five of us and my sister." He was still grinning as he said, "But she's neither little nor old. She's only fifty-six. And as fit and active as they come. Although, now that you've put the picture in my head, I can easily see her running after the five of us with her rolling pin."

Tasha grinned. "I like her already."

"She's going to love you."

Just like that, the light in Tasha's eyes died. Her movements robotic, she brought up the building app and said, "I've been playing with it a little already."

He wanted to take her hands in his and ask her what the hell had happened to make her so wary. Somehow, though, he managed to keep his hands to himself and his mouth shut.

Yes, he'd decided to risk his heart. But that didn't mean he wanted to destroy hers in the process. The fact that she was allowing him to help with her home was a good first step. He'd just have to hope she'd be ready to take the next step and confide in him soon.

Of course, that didn't stop him from wondering—was it something to do with her family? Was it a man? Or was it an issue with her job? He wondered about the *bumps* in Tasha's life just as much as he wondered about those maddening bumps his mother had alluded to.

Unfortunately, he was nowhere close to answers for either problem.

Turning his gaze to the computer screen, he saw that Tasha had digitally created the shell of the house, added walls and the bathroom with all the correct dimensions. "This looks great," he said. "We can start parsing out the kitchen. You want the sink under the window?"

She nodded. "And upper and base cabinets on this side. Then a tall pantry cupboard against this wall."

"Let's bring in the cabinets. We can adjust size—but it's cheaper if you use standard sizes—and we can move the pieces around." He clicked and popped in the sink.

"That's so cool." She looked at him. "You've really done something amazing here."

Amazing was her smooth skin, her silky hair beneath the ball cap with the phrase that kept giving him wild ideas. He hadn't realized the exquisite torture it would put him through when he bought it.

She began to select what she wanted, moving the pieces around. "I like these cabinets with the drawers in the base so I don't have to bend down to see what's at the back of the shelf. The carousel for the corner will utilize the space better." She was getting into it now. "And maybe it's better to put the tall pantry cupboard over here."

Her features came alive as she played in the app. She didn't need him; she had it all figured out on her own. But he loved watching her. Loved being with her.

For the next half hour, they moved cabinets and appliances like they were pieces on a chessboard. As the racket above increased, they drifted closer, their arms almost touching. He'd never been more aware of a woman, never more conscious of the curve of her lips when she talked or the music in her voice.

At one point, she reached for a piece of fruit in a bowl on the counter, taking a bite, leaving peach juice on her lips. He had the wildest urge to lick it off. But she did it before he could, the sight of her tongue driving him to the brink.

He wanted to grab her hand, suck the peach juice off her fingers and from her lips. Wanted to kiss her until she begged him for *more*.

Instead, he talked about counters and backsplash tile and range hoods, all the while drinking in her excitement as though it were an elixir.

This was the real Tasha Summerfield—he'd learned her last name today when she'd made her purchases at his store. She was enthused about life, about new projects. She loved to talk, loved exchanging ideas. She would have been the girl who always raised her hand in class, the cheerleader of her study group, the one voted most likely to succeed.

Yet here she was, living alone in a run-down cabin in the woods.

Again, he thought as a dark cloud shrouded his head, nothing added up.

"I love it!" She was practically beaming, her face lit by her excitement. "I can't wait to get it all installed." She looked down, holding out her hands as if she knew they were capable of anything.

All he could think was that he wanted her hands on him. And his on her. Touching her everywhere.

Driving her absolutely *wild*.

"You suggested so many things I never would have thought of," she went on, seemingly oblivious to the heat building to a fever pitch inside him. "I know you said to stop saying thank you, but I just can't stop. *Thank you, thank you, thank you!*"

In her exuberance, she threw her arms around him, and it was so natural that he knew it was another clue to the woman she'd been trying so desperately to keep hidden away.

He wanted her to let out her true self, to break the bonds of fear that had made her run away from her life and her career. He wanted to set her free.

And he wanted her to be *his*.

Time seemed to stop as he instinctively pulled her against him. There was nothing but her soft curves nestled close, the sweetness of her breath against his ear, her silky hair caressing him. He raised a hand, pulling back far enough to stroke his fingers along her chin. Her eyes were a radiant blue, as bright as the real Tasha struggling to get out.

Everything stilled around them, even the hammering above. He let his gaze rest on her lips—a sweet offering, lush, kissable. Nothing on earth could have stopped him, not even his own chivalry, as he lowered his head for that first glorious taste of her.

She tasted like the peach she'd eaten just a little while ago, sweet and ripe and luscious.

She could have stopped him, lifted her head, ended it all. He prayed she wouldn't.

Then she angled her head.

And consumed him.

★ ★ ★

Daniel's kiss lit a wildfire inside her.

His muscles were rock hard, and she swore she'd never felt anything so wonderful in all her life as she kissed him with everything she'd buried deep inside all these months.

It was a kiss like no other. It was fire and it was light. It was a spot in heaven far from reality. It was sweet sensation and sinful desire.

In that glorious moment, he was hers completely. And she was his.

She kissed him until she couldn't breathe. Her legs moved restlessly, wanting to wrap around him, feel him, every hard line of him. His arms were strong, but his hold gentle. She could stay this way forever.

But she'd forgotten that she couldn't have forever. Not anymore.

Too late, she remembered exactly who she was: Natasha Summerfield, daughter of a con man on a national scale.

She didn't deserve such a beautiful, perfect kiss. She didn't deserve Daniel. Or his friends. She didn't deserve their help. She didn't deserve how nice they were to her.

They thought she was just some poor girl who'd been foolish enough to buy this wreck of a cabin.

But she knew better.

"I'm sorry," she whispered, forcing herself to break their kiss and trying to push back. "I didn't mean to get carried away."

He didn't let go, his arm a band around her. "Don't say you're sorry. Because I'm not."

He was so close and felt so good. God help her, she

wanted to start that kiss all over again and never stop. "You don't really know me."

"I know enough."

"Please." She didn't honestly know what she was asking for. *Please let me go? Please kiss me again?*

All she knew was that she couldn't bear for him to discover the truth about her. How his gaze would surely change. How the coldness would descend.

She felt dirty for ever having allowed Eric to put his hands on her. How could she let Daniel touch her after that?

"Please let me go," she whispered. It was the right thing to do. The best thing to do.

The only thing.

But it hurt so badly when his arms finally slipped away.

"What's wrong, Tasha? You can confide in me. I won't hurt you, I promise."

She was the one who would hurt him, who was already doing it as she told him her first bald-faced lie. "Nothing's wrong. I just don't know how I'm possibly going to pay you back for everything you have done for me."

He frowned. "There's no price. You don't owe me anything."

She felt nauseated now, hating that she'd just de-based their kiss by making it sound like nothing more than *payment*. "I don't mean a price. I..." She was making a mess of it. An even bigger mess than she already had. "I'd better check the puppies. They've been alone a long time."

"Tasha."

But she was already running, away from everything she'd ever wanted.

And could never hope to have.

Chapter Fourteen

Tasha's heart nearly burst with loss as she picked up Darla and stroked her soft fur. How she longed to return to Daniel, to beg him to forgive her, to kiss her again. To hold her.

"But I can't allow this thing between us to grow," she told the puppy, her only confidante. "No matter how much I want it to."

Daniel wasn't her only danger either. His friends—his foster brothers—were as well. They loved him, cared about him, and he would clearly do anything for them. She respected them, liked them for their humor, their confidence, for the loving way they talked about their families, including their foster mother and father.

His family was yet another reason why she couldn't get any closer. She didn't deserve to be a part of a loving, perfect family like his. And she certainly didn't deserve Daniel.

Carefully, she put Darla back into the pen to play with her brothers. Daniel had gone up on the roof to work with his friends, and she couldn't hang out with the puppies all day, doing nothing while the men did all the labor. There was a ton she still had to do inside. By herself, where she could think things through without being distracted by Daniel's proximity, by his scent, by the heat of his body as they worked side by side.

As she fixed yet another hole in the flooring, Evan entered the house, obviously wanting to talk to her.

"I saw you and Daniel working on the computer earlier," he said in a deceptively easy voice. "How are the plans coming?"

Icy fear washed through her. Fifteen minutes ago, Tasha would have launched into an excited soliloquy on the great ideas Daniel had given her, how marvelous his design app was. But now she was consumed by one question: *What else had Evan noticed?*

He must have seen them kissing. Otherwise, he wouldn't be here, no doubt prepared to tell her to leave his friend alone.

"Fine," she said, her voice trembling over the four letters. She stood on shaky legs, hooking her hammer into its loop on her tool belt.

Evan folded his arms over his chest and leaned against the wall like he didn't plan on going anywhere soon. "I have a confession to make."

Her stomach did a pitch and roll as though she were on a ferry in bad weather. His next words were a no-brainer, so she should have been able to steel herself against them. Yet there was no way to stop them piercing her like a knife.

"What's that?" she asked, her heart racing so fast

she felt lightheaded.

"First," Evan said, "you should know that when we were kids, Daniel was always the first to come to our defense with the bigger kids. He's the kind of guy who's always got your back, no questions asked."

She swallowed, her throat sticking as if she hadn't had a drink of water in a year. "He's a good guy," she said around the rising bile.

"The best," he agreed, "which is why I worry about him." He held her gaze. "Especially around women."

He meant especially around *her*.

"Is everything all right with you, Tasha?" Evan let the question hang when she didn't answer. "Because it seems like something's wrong."

Her blood roared so loudly in her ears that she understood what he said only by reading his lips.

"I can't help wondering why you're here in Tahoe all by yourself. And why you're so reluctant to let us help." Evan pulled out his phone, slid his finger over the screen, and turned it so she could see.

She'd never be able to take another full breath in her life. Her lungs had stopped working. Her heart had stopped beating.

"I saw your name on the purchase orders for the roofing material you picked up today," he explained. "And I remembered a story I'd heard about two men named Reggie and Drew Summerfield who ran a resort scam, a father and son con-man team. Plus a third partner whose name isn't mentioned." He paused for several long seconds that made her squirm. "Do you know them, Tasha?"

What he didn't say screamed at her. *Are you the third partner?*

She should have hated him for spying on her. But she understood exactly why he had. To protect his friend, his brother.

The way no one had ever protected her. Or her brother.

She wanted to shout, *I'm not the third partner.* But the denial got stuck in her throat. Just because she hadn't known about the scam didn't mean she hadn't been an integral part of it. Her work on the website had lied to all those people just the way her father's smooth salesmanship had.

When she didn't answer, he added, "I wanted to get the story from you first. If there is one."

They both knew that he already had enough of the story to damn her. "I won't hurt Daniel, I promise." She heaved a sigh. "But my past...it belongs to me."

Saying nothing was probably worse than coming right out and saying Reggie Summerfield was her father and Drew was her brother and that she'd built the website for their scam. And yet she *still* couldn't manage to get the words out of her mouth, even ones that would have made it clear to Evan that she hadn't been an active partner in the con.

She could only contemplate where she'd run to next. She'd arrived in the mountains with one bag. She would leave the same way.

And Daniel would be saved from her lies, her secrets, and her past.

Evan regarded her, his eyes dark and assessing, the way they'd been from the moment he'd met her. "I'm sorry I had to ask. But Daniel's my brother." He shoved the phone into his pocket and left.

She was sorry too. So very sorry that she'd brought all this to Daniel's doorstep.

The only way to fix it now was to leave. Even if it killed everything inside her.

* * *

Tasha sat on the floor, alone in the house, for what seemed like forever. If she said good-bye to Daniel, he would try to convince her to stay—but she couldn't remain without telling him the truth. Yet she wouldn't be able to stand the way he looked at her once he knew. Her only choice was to sneak away after the guys had left for the day. Now, though, she'd say her good-byes to the puppies.

Outside, hunkering down by the pen Daniel had made for them, Tasha stuck the tips of her fingers through the chicken wire. Darla waddled over to lick her.

"It's okay, little one," Tasha said in a shaky voice. "You're going to be fine. Daniel will take care of you, I know he will."

Darla plopped over sideways, surely the cutest

puppy in the entire world. Not to be outdone by his sister, Spanky bounded over, followed by Froggy. They licked her fingers exuberantly, then began wrestling with each other, Spanky ending up on top as he mouthed his brother's face in friendly abandon.

"I'll miss you all." Tears slid down Tasha's cheeks. "I'm sorry I have to leave you."

Oh, how she would miss them all. The puppies. The Mavericks.

Daniel.

It had been only a few days, but they'd been momentous. She'd gotten attached so fast and had come to think of this cabin as someplace special, even if it was a wreck. Daniel had helped her envision what her house could be. What *home* could be.

What being with him would be.

Because *he* was what truly made it home.

The heartbreak of losing it all—of losing him—would last forever.

Evan would tell them her story, if he hadn't already. He'd say she hadn't denied anything. Daniel would understand why she'd gone.

Staring at the puppies, she wanted to smile at their antics. But looking into a future without these loving, furry little creatures—without Daniel—she didn't know if she would ever really smile again.

With every minute that ticked by since Evan had shared his discovery, she couldn't stop asking herself— how could she possibly atone for her family's sins?

Three months alone up here hadn't accomplished it. So what would?

She'd never told anyone about the resort scam, not a single one of her friends. She hadn't needed to tell the investigators; they'd already known as much as she did. Even with Evan just now, she hadn't been able to speak the words aloud.

Maybe, it suddenly hit her, part of true atonement was confessing what you'd done to people you cared about. Like a twelve-step program, where you had to state your problem before you could start to get better.

She'd run away from her friends, from her work, her life, because she feared they would blame her for her part in the scam. But ultimately, was hiding out here any different than what her father and brother were doing, lying low until they could strike again?

She'd been afraid of Daniel finding out, of what he would think of her. Of what his friends would think of her.

But telling Daniel, telling them all, finally coming clean—maybe *that* was atonement. Confession. Facing up to what you'd done. Admitting it aloud to the people who were important to you.

Was it possible that all along she'd been running from the one thing she really needed to do?

Yes, she realized. That was exactly what she'd been doing, running and hiding so that she didn't have to face anyone at all.

She felt the rightness of her epiphany in the fear

that clogged her chest. She was terrified of confession. And wasn't that the very reason she needed to do it? Because she had to show she was not the same as her family, that she could face her mistakes.

She had to stop hiding out. She had to stop running from her past. From her family secrets.

No matter the cost to her pride.

Or to her heart.

Returning to the cabin, she was glad everyone was on the roof—including Daniel—so she could shower and change, not back into overalls and a baseball cap, but into the jeans she used to wear, jeans that had grown loose on her, and a purple top. She needed to make her confession as the woman she'd been when she stood in her father's office, dressed the way she used to when she was the person who, no matter how unwittingly, had been a part of her family's scam.

It was tempting to stay holed up in her bedroom, to delay facing the music just a little longer. But she'd been a coward long enough.

It was finally time to do one brave thing.

Hopefully, it would prepare her to keep on being brave, once she'd made it through today in one piece.

If she made it through today.

When she emerged from her bedroom, she was surprised to find Daniel standing in the living room. His eyes widened when he saw her in something other than work clothes for once. "You look beautiful."

"Daniel—"

But he wouldn't let her say what she needed to. "I tried to let you go, told myself to give you space, but every second I was up there hammering, I was thinking about you. About our kiss. And how you ran."

"I'm finally ready to stop running." Ready, yes, but still petrified of what he'd think of her.

A smile curved his lips. "That's exactly what I wanted to hear."

She held her hands up to keep him at a distance. "Actually, I'm sure it's not."

He ignored her cues to back off, taking her hands in his. "Whatever you've been so worried about, I'm sure it's nowhere near as bad as you think."

She was trembling like the leaves on the aspens outside. "I'm guessing Evan hasn't told you. He found an article on the Internet about my family."

Fire flashed in Daniel's eyes. "I told him not to butt in."

"Don't be angry with him for looking me up. He cares about you. That's why he did it."

"I understand why," Daniel said. "But I know my own feelings for you. And nothing he says is going to change them."

Her heart wanted to soar. But Daniel didn't know the truth, and once he did, everything would dive-bomb instead. "I don't want to come between you and one of your brothers."

"That's one thing the Mavericks never do," he told her. "We're there for each other through thick and thin, pain and heartache."

That's why they were such good men. She was certain there was a huge story there, for each of them
separately and the group as a whole. But she had her
own story to tell.

Finally.

She didn't start with any ice-breaking explanations.
She simply laid out the truth. "My father and brother
are con men." She made herself say each word, even
though they tasted like poison on her tongue. "They
bilked millions of dollars out of people for a resort that
doesn't exist. And they got caught." She was sure
Daniel would drop her hands, but his grip only tightened. "I worked with them. I didn't know what they
were doing, but I designed the website they used to
draw in their victims." She could no longer look at
him. "I was a complete idiot. I didn't question anything. I was just happy that they wanted to include me
in their fabulous new project." Sarcasm edged each
word.

Daniel didn't wait a beat. "You didn't do anything
wrong, Tasha." His voice was steady. Strong. And
utterly certain. "It wasn't your fault. You didn't know."

She couldn't let him make excuses for her. "I
should have known. Because the cons didn't start when
I was an adult. They'd been going on since I was a kid.
That's why we had to move all the time. My father had
to run before he got caught, taking the money he'd
bilked out of his investors. I was stupid and blind. I

never questioned anything. I just enjoyed our fancy houses and private schools and cars and vacations."

He held on when she would have pulled away. "Even if you had figured it out as a kid, you couldn't have stopped it. That's not a kid's job."

She squeezed her eyes shut, remembering every time they'd had to leave, every completed con under her father's belt. "That's still the family I come from. They're my bad genes. I went to college on money they stole from other people. My dad bought me my first car with money he ripped off. I helped them scam unwitting investors with a beautiful website that made everything look legitimate when it was totally fake."

"You aren't your family." Certainty underlay his words.

The breath she took hurt like ice crystals filling her lungs. "But I went along with their lies. I loved my father and brother and believed in them."

"That makes you a loving daughter and sister. Not the person responsible for their lies to you and everyone else."

"Even now—" She had to finish her confession, no matter how he tried to minimize her crimes. "Even knowing that my brother was part of it, I still want to believe he's a good person. I want to believe that he hated the things he was doing." Daniel swept away a tear, and his touch was so beautiful, so totally unconditional, that she felt her heart crushed under the weight of his acceptance. "There's more," she whispered.

"Whatever you say, I'm not going to believe you're a bad person."

But once he heard the rest of it, she knew he would. "My father introduced me to a man—his business partner. And I was charmed. I thought Eric was wonderful. I thought he cherished me. Truly cared for me. But everything he told me, everything he did and said, was a lie."

"I'm so sorry." Daniel wrapped his arm around her shoulders, tucking her into his body as if he could erase the pain she felt and the mistakes she'd made.

"I don't miss my ex, I swear I don't. But I feel like the dumbest person in the world. A total fool who helped the three of them dot the i's and cross the t's on their cons until the moment they needed to run."

"Leaving you to fend for yourself." The words were barely more than a growl from Daniel.

"My father wanted me to run too. Before the police started asking questions. But I talked to the investigators. I answered everything, and they let me go as though I hadn't done anything wrong." Her voice dropped to almost nothing. "Then I came here."

"I'm so glad you're here, Tasha. So, so glad."

Daniel's words snapped the final thread of her control. Her tears soaked his shirt as he pulled her into the shelter of his arms, enveloping her.

Chapter Fifteen

Daniel held her tight for long minutes, absorbing her sobs until they softened into sniffles.

"Hey, look at me." He kept his voice gentle as he tipped up Tasha's chin. She'd stopped crying, but her lashes were still damp, the rims of her eyes reddened.

"I didn't mean to cry all over you," she said in a voice still thick with tears. "I just needed to tell you the whole truth, with nothing left out."

The pain of what she'd experienced clenched in his gut. Yet he was grateful that she'd finally given him her trust, confided her deepest secrets. Each of the Mavericks knew just how deep into the darkness family secrets could drag you if you let them.

"Your guilt, your belief in your culpability—those aren't the truth," he said. "You're not to blame, Tasha. Not for any of it."

She blinked, slowly, finally looking up. "It *is* the truth, Daniel. Everything I told you."

"Not the part where you load the blame on yourself, taking responsibility for not seeing through your father's lies."

His heart hurt for the loss of her illusions about her family. Hell, it made his chest tight just to skirt around the issue of possible bumps in the road between his mother and father, so he could understand how much her family's long con must have devastated her. But to blame herself? He couldn't accept that. He *wouldn't* accept it.

"We're not the products of our parents, with no ability to change. We don't need to live with their stigma. And we don't ever have to be like them. We can be better than they are and rise above our circumstances."

Every one of his friends had come from a hell created by their parents. That's why his mom and dad had taken them in. And still, the Mavericks had risen far above their backgrounds—and their bad genes, as Tasha had called it—not just in terms of money, but in their integrity, their loyalty, their kindness toward others.

"You wanted to see only the good in your dad." He cupped her cheek, stroking her skin with his thumb, the contact necessary to his entire being. "That's natural, even admirable. Children are born having faith that their parents will take care of them, watch out for them, love them. But if your parents blow it—that's not your fault."

"Can't you see how weak I was?" she insisted. "Living in la-la land where everyone is good and no one ever does anything simply for their own gain and at the expense of others."

"My mother always looks for the good in people," he countered, "and she's the farthest thing from weak."

"I didn't mean—"

He laid his finger on her lips, reminding himself of her sweet taste, how good she felt in his arms. "I know you didn't mean anything against her. I'm trying to show you that it's okay to give people a chance instead of judging them too quickly. Mom believes you have to see the good in people and everything around you. Or life is just misery. Even though she's wrong sometimes—because not everyone *is* good—I admire that about her more than I can say." He caressed the fine hair at Tasha's temple. "And I admire that about you too."

"I bet your mom never met anyone who did things as evil as my father."

He almost snorted. "Oh yes, she has." But he wouldn't tell Tasha about Whitney right now. Or the other Mavericks' parents. Or the selfish punk who'd run Jeremy off the road and left him with brain damage. This moment needed to be all about Tasha. The rest could come later. "You've got to remember that your *father* did those things, not you. All you did was miss the clues about him. That's not evil. It doesn't make you bad."

"I just don't know if I'll ever see it that way." Her words were harsh, full of pain.

And they broke his heart.

He couldn't make her see the truth in one blinding flash, but he needed her to understand what *he* saw when he looked at her. "You're loving and caring. You're loyal. You still love your brother and believe there has to be a reason he took the actions he did."

Tasha was a pure soul, even if she didn't know it. She was Maverick material.

He leaned his forehead against hers. "My mom is my hero. You've probably already figured that out. And you have so many of the same qualities. She would adore you."

Tasha shifted against him, her eyes squeezed tightly shut. "I've been so afraid of what you'd say when you learned the truth. How you'd hate me."

He ached that her words clearly proved she still didn't believe him. "I could never hate you." He kissed her cheek. "I couldn't care about someone who callously hurt others." He kissed her eyelid, tasting the lingering salt of her tears. "I would only want to help someone who can't resist rescuing puppies." He kissed the tip of her nose and slid his fingers into her hair. "Not to mention someone who loves my do-it-yourself videos."

She laughed softly, a sound he'd been desperately waiting for, and he took her parted lips with his. What he couldn't make her hear with words, he tried to say with his kiss.

It was a kiss of acceptance and forgiveness.

A kiss to say he didn't give a damn about her family

or what they'd done.

Their first kiss had moved the earth like a 7.0 quake. Tasha's finally opening herself up to him, so beautifully, so completely, had been more than anything he could have hoped for. Better than any fantasy.

But this kiss was beyond his wildest dreams—pure, sweet, unconditional emotion, laced with sizzling heat.

Tasha's hands fisted in his shirt as if it were the only way she could remain on her feet as he cupped her nape in his hand and plundered her mouth the way he wanted to plunder her body. He forgot they were standing in the middle of her living room. All he desired was her body against his, to taste her, to show her with his hands, mouth, and soul that her past was immaterial.

Only the beautiful person she was inside mattered.

Her fingers loosened and she rose on her tiptoes to wrap her arms around him, her breasts pressed to his chest. She smelled like a fresh rain shower and tasted as sweet as fruit. Her hair fell in a silk web over his hands and arms, caressing him like the sweep of her fingers across his skin.

He lost himself in her sweetness, kissing her until his head swam, being kissed by her until he couldn't feel the floor beneath his feet.

Nothing existed but Tasha.

He would have kissed her forever if, behind them, someone hadn't cleared his throat.

★ ★ ★

Tasha felt lightheaded, not just from that glorious kiss, or from realizing Daniel's friends had been standing in her shell of a living room watching them for who knew how long.

No, she was dizzied by the miracle that *Daniel didn't hate her.*

She'd worried about his reaction for so long and so hard, convinced he'd think the worst of her. The fact that he hadn't was like drinking champagne bubbles so fast they went straight to her head.

He hadn't walked away from her in horror. He hadn't withdrawn the help he'd offered.

Instead, he'd said her family's crimes weren't her fault.

Then he'd dazzled her with his kiss.

She still didn't feel she deserved his unconditional acceptance. Nor did it feel right to love anything half as much as she loved Daniel's kisses.

She had so much to make up for—and so much more courage to find within herself. Which was why she had to step away from him now, though every cell in her body craved his closeness. It was why a kiss that beautiful could never happen again.

But at least she wasn't living under a cloud of lies anymore.

Now, she had another test, another act of bravery. She had to face his friends' reactions to the truth. Evan certainly hadn't been pleased when he'd found the damning evidence about her father and brother. He couldn't be anything but furious to find her wrapped so cozily around Daniel.

As though he could read her mind, Daniel tightened his hold on her, not allowing even an inch of space between them.

"It's not their business," he said softly. "It's your story and your right to keep it to yourself."

"I need to tell them everything, just like I told you." She'd been weak for so long, she had to step up now, no matter how scary it was.

"We're heading down to the big house to get some dinner and wondered if you two wanted to come along." Sebastian's comment was the world's most subtle way of saying, *It would be nice if one of you told us what the hell is going on.*

Tasha's heart was beating like hummingbird wings, but she pushed the words out. "I've just told Daniel who I am and why I'm here. Now I want to tell all of you." She looked straight at Evan. "You're his best friends, and I know how much you care about him. I didn't set out to hurt anyone—"

"Tasha." Daniel's voice was warm and gentle. "They're not going to judge you for what your family did."

But she couldn't let him speak for his friends. Without further preamble, she told them everything, exactly as she'd told Daniel.

When she finally took a breath, Evan closed the distance to stand in front of her. "I spent the past hour up on the roof knowing there had to be more to your story than what I found online. But it was my own history that made me paint things in black and white, without even knowing what the hell I was talking about." His eyes were shadowed, anger with himself marring the curve of his mouth. "Forgive me for being an ass, Tasha."

Before she could tell him he didn't need her for-giveness for anything—who could blame him for wanting to protect his friend?—the others chimed in.

"We never thought you were anything but good," said Will.

From Matt, "You don't owe us explanations. Ari and Noah will love you."

And a heartfelt, "Come here and give me a hug," from Sebastian, who, with his arms gentle and accept-ing around her, whispered, "Sorry we interrupted right when things were getting good between you and Daniel."

The Mavericks were the men she wished her father could have been. The men she wished her brother actually was.

All the while, Daniel stood tall beside her, believing in her.

His unconditional acceptance—and that of his friends—blurred her eyes with tears all over again. She'd dropped her guard and nothing bad had happened. She'd told the truth, and they hadn't snarled like rabid dogs the way Eric had.

She still had so much more to make up for, but she was proud of taking the first step, of confessing her greatest faults to people she respected.

There was so much more to do, a long road of actions she had to take, but first, she needed the Mavericks to know how grateful she was. "I can never thank you all enough for everything you've done." For working on her house. And, more important, for pardoning her terrible mistakes. "I appreciate your help from the bottom of my heart."

Daniel took her hand in his, squeezing her fingers lightly, spreading his warmth through her. "You've got the Mavericks behind you, Tasha." He grinned. "Whether you want us or not."

"I'm starving." Matt's stomach growled right on cue. "Steak for dinner sound good to everyone?"

Tasha couldn't believe they'd forgiven her and, just like that, moved on to practical matters like food and who'd lost the extra box of roofing nails and if the weather would hold out until the new roof was finished tomorrow.

But instead of following them, Tasha said, "I'll be along in a little bit. Don't wait on dinner for me, okay?"

Daniel got that stubborn look, the one she was starting to know quite well, readying himself to insist on staying with her. Until she whispered, "I'm not going to run. I promise. There's just something I need to do." She gave him a small but heartfelt smile.

He left with obvious reluctance—and no small measure of concern for her creasing the corners of his eyes. As soon as the men were walking down the mountain toward his house, Tasha went to her laptop.

She hadn't been into her email for so long that she fumbled her password a couple of times. But if she was brave enough to tell Daniel—and the Mavericks as well—then she couldn't stop there.

It was time, long past time, to find out where Drew and her father had gone.

She sent her brother a quick email. Moments later, she got a domain notice saying the email address didn't exist. Just as she'd thought. She sent a brief note to Barbara, her father's receptionist, saying the usual, *Hi, hope all is well, heard from my brother or my dad? Thanks.* Who else could she contact? She trolled her history, finding a group email from her brother that included addresses for a couple of his friends. She sent queries their way too. A polite opening, then, *Heard anything from my brother?*

She stared at the screen, thinking, thinking. Who else? She didn't bother with either of the investigators who'd talked to her. If they'd tracked down her father and Drew, they'd already be in jail. But hadn't there been a lawyer her father had brought in? Tasha pressed her fingers to her temples to try to squeeze a name out of her brain. Nothing came.

Barbara might remember. As soon as the receptionist emailed her back—*if* she emailed back—Tasha would ask her. Heck, Barbara might know lots of other names to try.

For now, though, Tasha couldn't think of anyone else, which made her realize how pitifully little she knew about her family.

Her heart was beating fast and her fingers trembled slightly on the keys of her laptop as she waited for someone to reply. But her inbox remained glaringly empty. She'd have to wait, hoping someone would have a trail she could follow.

Yet despite the failure to receive any answers, it was good to finally do something constructive. She wasn't running, she wasn't hiding. She was being proactive.

And the person she had to thank for that was Daniel. Because without his touch, his kiss, or his belief in her, she might never have found the courage.

Chapter Sixteen

Two days later, Tasha and Daniel stood together in his driveway, waving as Will backed the SUV out. "Good-bye," Tasha called. "Thank you for everything."

The Mavericks had decided to leave early on Monday so they could spend the rest of the holiday with their loved ones at home. They weren't taking Spanky or Froggy yet, agreeing not to split up the puppies until they were a little older. But Tasha had sent the guys off with a hearty lunch packed in Harper's picnic basket.

When the SUV disappeared around a curve in the road, she turned to smile at Daniel, and the beauty that was a glow around her made his heart leap in his chest. "I'm going to miss them," she said. "And not just for putting on my new roof. I really like your friends."

"They're good guys." The absolute truth, however? He wouldn't miss them today. Not when all he'd craved since Saturday evening was to have Tasha to himself.

He'd walked her back to her place Saturday night, but instead of sharing another kiss, she'd evaded him completely, with yesterday being a repeat.

Yet, no matter how much he wanted her, no matter how frustrated he was in his cold, lonely bed, he didn't want to make a mistake by pushing things too fast. She'd been hurt badly by her scum of an ex and by her father's betrayal. In her position, he wouldn't want to leap into a new relationship too quickly either. Especially when they hadn't been alone since she'd told him the truth about her family. There'd been no chance to really talk. She was still wary, holding back, balking at outward displays of affection in front of his friends. He wanted to learn so much more about her, more details about her life. He wanted to get to know her, *really* know her.

Anyone who knew Daniel also understood that he'd been driven his whole life by one thing: determination. He'd been determined to make it out of the slums. He'd been determined to grow his business to the point where he could take his parents—and the rest of his family—with him. Now, he wanted nothing more than to make Tasha laugh, to bring her completely out of her shell and, most of all, to forgive herself.

Daniel Spencer *never* failed once he set his mind on something.

And his mind was most definitely set on Tasha.

After her confession to Daniel and his friends, he and the guys had talked privately about her situation. The Mavericks were ready and raring to track down her family, including the bastard ex-boyfriend. They certainly had the resources to do it. But in his opinion, only Tasha had the right to track—and confront—her family.

Of course, the guys couldn't stand to do absolutely nothing, so for now they'd agreed to search out victims of the scam and make sure all of them received restitution. Daniel had already called the Mavericks' private investigator to get that ball rolling. He'd let Tasha know about it if and when there were results.

Yet again, he'd considered telling the Mavericks about his strange conversations with his mother. Only, was there really anything to tell them? No matter how he tried to downplay it, they'd probably put a full-court press on Mom, trying to wring out what was bothering her. They'd feel duty-bound to help her in any way they could. But was that the right thing for her, when she seemed so anxious about whatever the problem was? So he'd decided to say nothing for the time being.

"I have to thank you too." Tasha broke into his thoughts, her voice earnest. "I don't even know where to begin."

"I've enjoyed every moment. We all have." The rest of the materials she'd purchased had been delivered yesterday, but as much as he liked working with hammer and nails, it would do them both a heck of a lot of good to get away for a little while. "You know what we need to do today?"

"Yes," she said. "You've done so much to help me with my place, I want to help you with yours."

It was a generous offer, one he'd happily take her

up on later—not only for her excellent building skills, but because he'd take any opportunity to be near her. For now, though, he waved it away with a better idea. "A hike and a picnic."

"*A hike and a picnic?*" She said the words the way she might have said, *You want me to eat big hairy spiders for lunch?*

He couldn't help laughing, but he wasn't going to let her hide out in her cabin a minute longer. She enjoyed the work as much as he did, but there was so much more to life, and he wanted to remind her of it.

"We both deserve time off." He led her into his kitchen, where he had a backpack and water bottles waiting. "Plus, I already packed lunch for us. I'm sure you don't want my efforts to go to waste."

She looked suspiciously at the bag. "Please tell me you didn't pack your secret stash of caviar in there."

He slapped a hand to his chest. "Words to strike at a billionaire's heart," he joked. The guys had talked up Will's excellent imported caviar, but Tasha had scrunched her nose. "Even though I know you'll love caviar when you finally try it"—her eyes widened at the word *when*, but he wanted her to get used to the idea that this feeling growing between them didn't have an end date—"if I promise there's no caviar on the menu today, will you agree to come hiking with me?"

She thought about it for a moment. "I wouldn't want all your hard picnic-making work to go to waste, but we could always eat it when we take a break later today."

"Work, work, work." A smile creased his lips simply from the sweetness of looking at her. "Aren't you ever lazy for just a little while?"

"No," she said. But her eyes lit up, and suddenly she was laughing. "And you never give up on your goals either, do you?"

"No, I don't."

He wouldn't give up on his goal to win her heart, that was for sure.

She held up her hands in surrender. "All right, you win. But what about the puppies?"

"They'll be fine in the pen in the shade. The hike to Grass Lake is too far for them. Plus, we've got to cross some streams. We can leave extra water and plenty of kibble to tide them over until we get back. You're going to have a great time," he promised her. "I won't let you down."

With those words, he was asking her to trust him. He understood it was a huge deal for her, with so many more implications than a mere hike. After all, her family had let her down in the worst of ways.

But Daniel meant every word, and he refused to hold back any more than absolutely necessary. Not when Tasha was everything he'd given up hope of finding—smart, independent, compassionate, and oh-so-sexy.

"All right," she said at last. "I'll put on my hiking

boots."

At her house, she plopped on a pink ball cap, pulling her hair through and letting her ponytail cascade down her back. His fingers itched to tangle themselves in the silk.

He laughed when she turned, pointing at the stitching. "That's a good sign."

Tracing the letters, she smiled, turning his heart as soft as the center of a chocolate crème. *"Not adulting today."* She shrugged. "Very millennial, I know."

"I for one am glad you're not *adulting* today." He wanted her carefree and happy, without the shadows she'd lived under for so long.

They took care of the puppies, then hit the trailhead, climbing to the lake along the fire road, passing waterfalls gushing with the last of the snowmelt. She walked slightly in front of him, and he enjoyed the mesmerizing sway of her ponytail and the strength in her calves.

"You're a great hiker."

"Thanks," she said with a smile. "Dad and Drew and I used to—" Her smile fell halfway through her sentence. "I've always loved hiking," she said instead of whatever family tidbit she'd been about to reveal.

He wished she'd feel comfortable sharing more, but who was he to judge when he hadn't shared his concerns about his conversations with his mother with anyone? Yet he still didn't feel it was right to saddle Tasha with his stuff when he didn't even have his facts straight.

"Anyway," she continued, "I've been dying to know, how did the Mavericks meet their wives?"

He saw the question for what it was, a way to take the focus off her and her family. But his answer could, if used skillfully, draw her out. Let her get to know him until she didn't notice she was revealing more about herself too.

He wasn't giving up. Not by a long shot.

★ ★ ★

They talked the entire time they hiked up the trail. And Tasha loved all the stories about his family.

"Will met Harper through her brother, Jeremy, who was majorly into Will's classic car collection. But honestly, I think Will fell for him first. He's a great kid. So happy all the time." He told her about Jeremy's accident, and her heartstrings twanged for the boy. "Will and Harper got married on New Year's Eve, and Jeremy gave her away. It even made me cry." He mimed wiping his eyes.

"What about Sebastian?" Tasha had already heard what a fabulous artist Charlie Ballard was. Sebastian's praise had been nonstop. Tasha had looked up her work online, and it was truly stunning—as was Charlie herself.

"He was looking for an artist to create something for his new headquarters. He went crazy for her work—but he totally went off the deep end for Charlie herself. Plus, you've got to love her mom, Francine. That little lady walks a mile a day despite her crippling arthritis. She's amazing."

Tasha adored listening to him—to the love that laced his words, to his deep, beautiful voice that made something sing inside her. She'd loved her father and brother, but nothing had ever seemed as exquisite as Daniel's heartfelt stories about his family.

Thinking about her own family reminded her she needed to send out more emails. Though having heard nothing themselves, Barbara and Drew's friends had written back to give her more names to contact. She had so much more to do, but for today, she would let herself bask in the sweetness of being out in nature with Daniel.

"And Matt?" she prompted him, pushing back the bill of her cap as she glanced over her shoulder at him. The day was warm, but not grindingly hot.

"He's done such a great job of raising his son alone. Noah is the best. He's so smart, so interested in everything. Ari was his nanny, but she and Matt were always meant to be together, and they're getting married later this year."

"It's wonderful that they've all had such happy endings."

"It really is," he agreed. "Take Paige and Evan. They've known each other forever—she's his ex-wife's younger sister—and they're a match made in heaven. He actually met Paige first—it just took him a heck of a long time to recognize that real love was there in front of him all along."

She was glad Daniel's friends had all found a second chance. Even if she still wasn't sure she deserved one herself. After all, while most of the Mavericks' parents had been truly evil, the Mavericks themselves hadn't been complicit.

"The guys have come a long way from Chicago," Daniel said. "And let me tell you, none of them had it easy. They ran the gamut from alcoholic parents, to abuse, to abandonment."

Her foot slipped on a rock, but she caught herself before Daniel could touch her. They hadn't kissed again, not like that perfect moment in the cabin. Despite how marvelous he'd been about her huge confession, she was still on tenterhooks around him. Yet at the same time, she was so ready for his touch, his kiss, his heat, even as impossible as that was.

It was an effort to keep walking and talking instead of turning around and throwing herself at him. "You must have had it hard too, since you came from the same neighborhood."

"My parents made sure there was always enough love to go around and enough food on the table, even if we didn't have the finer things of life."

There were few men who would extol such virtues out loud. He wore his pride and love for his family like a suit of armor he never took off, a ward against anything bad. Yet there was the faintest shadow there as well, the same shadow that kept popping up whenever he talked about his parents. She wanted to press him, wanted to know more. But she knew how hard it was to open up all the way.

"And man," he said, "the Mavericks adore Lyssa. She's the little sister none of them had. They used to fight to see who got to take her to the park, not that it was much of a park. But if they saw any drug deals going down, they'd run out the offenders. Nothing was ever going to hurt Lyssa."

"You obviously love her very much."

"She's the apple of our eye, as my mom would say." He grinned wide with pride. "So pretty she makes men cry. And so smart. She graduated from college last year." Love brimmed in his voice, then with another big laugh, he added, "I pity any guy who falls for her, because he's going to have to run a gauntlet of Mavericks."

"Sounds terrifying."

"You should know, considering you've already faced them down. And they loved you."

"Evan didn't."

He reached for her hand. "He was wrong to make judgments before he knew all the facts. Now that he has them, he's on your side, Tasha. Just like I am."

When he looked at her like that, with such warmth and compassion—and something richer and deeper that she was afraid to acknowledge—she longed to throw herself at him and shower him with kisses.

But kissing him again would only bring more complications.

And more heartache when it was time to say goodbye.

Chapter Seventeen

"Tell me more about your mom and dad," Tasha asked as they waded through waist-high grass. "What made them want to foster so many boys?"

Every time he tried to shift the conversation to her, Tasha redirected it back to him and his family. But for the first time in his life, he was slightly uncomfortable talking about his parents. He used to be so sure their story was pure perfection from start to finish. Until his recent conversations with his mother had made him question that assumption.

He needed to talk with his mom again. Needed to find out if he was making something out of nothing. But he'd never felt the need to confront his mother about anything before. He'd always thought he was brave, bold. But every time he contemplated tackling the issue with his mom, a part of him questioned whether it would be easier just to go with the status quo, to tell himself it was his parents' business, not his.

At last, he answered Tasha. "I was about eleven or twelve when they started taking in my friends. We were already buddies in school, and everyone used to hang at my house. My parents were really easy to be around."

She took a bottle of water from the pack, drank for a long time, then licked her lips, leaving them glistening with invitation. "You mean because they were kind?"

"Yes." He grinned. "And because my mom makes the best chocolate chip cookies and brownies."

They passed a couple with two toddlers who were doing a great job climbing the hill.

"My parents loved kids," Daniel said. "They would have had more, but Lyssa didn't come along until I was ten. Then they started taking in the Mavericks."

Tasha turned, walking backward. "Were you okay with that?"

Before he could reply, she tripped on a rock and he grabbed her arm, steadying her with his body. "Whoa there." She was close enough for him to smell her hair and the saltiness of her skin. Close enough to see her pupils dilate. Close enough for everything inside him to turn to liquid fire. "You okay?" Daniel asked.

"I'm fine." But she definitely sounded breathless. "I should look where I'm going."

A part of him wished she wouldn't, if only to give him the excuse to hold her again. As it was, she felt too delicious to let go.

When he finally forced himself to ease away from her, the hot imprint of her body remained.

As they started climbing again, he answered her

question. "Whenever Mom and Dad wanted to bring one of the guys in permanently, they always sat me down and discussed it. They never forced anything on me. But even if I'd resisted sharing my parents' time with more than just Lyssa, I knew how bad, how brutal their home lives were. I couldn't wish that kind of existence on any of them. It tore my folks up when one of them came over with bruises. Or when they wouldn't talk because something bad had happened."

"I've never known anyone who cares about other people as much as you and your parents and friends do."

"What about your father?" He knew he was pushing her, but he hoped his sharing would make her feel she could do the same. "He wasn't cruel to you or your brother, was he?"

She started walking once more, head down, her expression hidden from him. "I always thought I was lucky to have such a great dad." Her sorrow was easy to hear, to feel, as she spoke. "But he never asked me or my brother how we felt about moving again."

Abruptly, she stopped in her tracks. "We've got to cross that?" She pointed to the log across a stream ahead. Swollen with the snowmelt, the water rushed below.

Before he could reply, however, she straightened her shoulders and started across. Walking as if it were a tightrope, one foot in front of the other, she teetered for a moment that made his breath catch, then found her balance again and darn near dashed the rest of the way.

He caught up on the other side. "I should have remembered about that crossing."

Taking him totally off guard, she cupped his cheek. "Actually, I like that you push me past my boundaries and think I can handle whatever you're going to dish out."

He knew *exactly* what he wanted to dish out—the kiss of a lifetime. But just then a couple of guys rounded the bend and passed them, practically leaping across the log as they headed down the trail.

"Showoffs," she muttered, making Daniel laugh, before she took off again at a fast clip.

Whether it was because she was trying to show the other hikers that she was every bit as good on the mountain, or because she'd sensed how badly Daniel wanted to kiss her and was intent on evading him, he didn't know.

The trail took a turn, and suddenly the alpine lake spread out before them, clear as glass, the reflection of the mountains like a painting on the water's surface.

"*Wow.*"

She didn't have to say more. Its majesty was why he loved this place. Why he wanted to bring her here today—so that she could experience the same peace and sense of awe it gave him.

He took her hand, needing to touch her again, and led her around to a flat rock where they could spread out their picnic. She seated herself, and he settled beside her, opening the pack to pull out an insulated bag with ice packs.

He tore off the lid on the first plastic tub. "Crackers." Another lid. "Local Brie and goat cheese." Then a smaller container. "Pepper jelly that's great with both."

She looked impressed. "And you said Matt was all about the food."

"He is." Daniel grinned. "But I can hold my own with the good stuff." Yet another tub contained fresh mango, papaya, grapes, and berries, plus a cheese knife and a jelly spoon. "Close your eyes, and try this." He sliced off creamy cheese, slathered it on a cracker, then topped it with pepper jelly. "Open up."

He fed her, touching her lips, letting her tongue caress his fingers. The sounds she made as she swallowed were ones he'd hear in his dreams.

"Wow."

"That's what you said about the lake."

She opened her eyes to gaze at him. "It goes for the food too."

And it went most especially for her.

"Wait, there's more." Tucking into the pack once more, he whisked out a split of champagne and two plastic flutes.

She laughed, a sound he'd loved since the first time he'd heard it. "You billionaires are too much," she teased.

"The champagne has nothing to do with my being

a billionaire. You deserve to be wined and dined by anyone you're with." He thought of the ex who'd lied to her and winced, waiting for the reminder to take the shine out of her.

But though something dark flashed through her gaze, for the first time, she didn't let it conquer her. Instead, she whispered, "Feed me more."

* * *

After the meal, sated with champagne, scrumptious cheese, and luscious fruit—and most of all, with the thought of how sweet Daniel had been to pull all of this together for her—Tasha was tempted to throw her fears to the winds and kiss him again.

When Eric had treated her to a fancy meal and a night out, it had only been to bolster his lies, not because he thought she deserved anything special.

Although Daniel was far more gorgeous and wealthy than her ex could ever hope to be, he was also real and sincere. Every cell in her body knew it.

But Daniel had to leave Fallen Leaf Lake eventually. Though he'd never given her the exact date of his departure, he wouldn't be able to stay in the mountains with her forever. His real life—his company and all the beautiful women who were surely a far better match for him—awaited his return.

Breaking into her maudlin thoughts, he announced, "Time to get wet."

"Wet?" She sounded like a nervous virgin, but she

couldn't help it. Whenever she was around Daniel her heart beat too hard and her breath came too fast.

"It'll be nice to soak our feet in the water for a bit. Unless—" A wicked light glinted in his eyes. "—you have other ideas?"

Did she ever. But she'd spent the past couple of days reminding herself over and over that she couldn't take more from Daniel than she already had, so instead of listing all the sinfully sexy ideas that immediately popped into her head, she chirped, "Soaking our feet is perfect!"

She nearly groaned at her hyperbole as she unlaced her hiking boots. Thankfully, putting her feet into the cool, crisp water cooled down both her embarrassment and her desperate desire. For a few minutes, at least.

"What a marvelous day," she said in as easy a voice as she could manage, considering she was reliving every luscious touch of his fingers on her lips as he'd fed her. He'd seduced her completely—he always did, even when they were both wearing tool belts and working side by side on her floorboards or her paneling.

God, it was hard not to give in to her feelings for him. But that didn't mean she couldn't enjoy this one perfect, sunny afternoon, did it? Would it be so wrong to let the pleasure of being with Daniel, even if only on a purely platonic level, fuel her for the difficult days ahead? Especially now that she'd decided to search for her father and brother and make absolutely certain they hadn't started another con. She should have looked for them months ago. But she'd been so shell-shocked that she'd hidden away in the mountains instead.

It wasn't until Daniel had come into her life and showed her that she was braver and stronger than she'd given herself credit for that she was finally able to take the steps she should have all along.

More grateful to him for his kindness and under-standing than she could ever express, she turned to smile at Daniel…and he gave her a smile so sweet, so sexy, so dazzling that her heart skipped like pebbles tossed across the lake.

★ ★ ★

Backlit as she was by the sunlight, Daniel had never seen a more gorgeous picture. Tasha's beauty should be immortalized on canvas and hung on museum walls for future generations. He'd ask Sebastian to sketch her.

He wanted to see her smile like that always. She had so much laughter inside her, so much sweetness and caring. So much loyalty.

Suddenly, she squealed and jerked her feet out of the water. "What was that?" She stared down into the depths.

He followed her gaze. And laughed. "It's the fish. They nibble." He wiggled his toes in the water and tiny fish darted away, slowly returning when he stilled again.

"You mean they're eating us? Like piranhas?" She hugged her knees to her chest, properly horrified.

"They're just nibbling," he explained through his laughter. "Looking for plankton or moss."

She proclaimed in mock indignation, "I don't have moss or plankton on my toes."

He leaned in close to whisper, "But I bet you still taste really, really good." Her cheeks instantly heated. "Now put your feet back in."

She wriggled her toes. "If I lose these, it will be your fault. And you'll owe me big time."

"All right, I'll owe you. What do you want?"

She gazed at him for an endless moment, and the laughter went out of him as she stole his breath.

"I'll tell you if they bite off my toes." Then she plunked her feet down in the water, splashing and scaring the fish away.

"You did that on purpose," he teased. "Be still and let them come back."

With her thigh pressed against his, the heat of her body arced through him like an electrical current. He laced their fingers, his thumb stroking patterns on her skin… and he nearly sighed with relief when she didn't pull away.

"Wait for it," he whispered as the fish circled closer.

"That is so cool." Her voice held such awe, as if she were witnessing a miracle. "It's like…" She bit her bottom lip, thinking hard. "Like feathers tickling your toes. Or dragonfly wings against your cheek. Or champagne bubbles bursting in your mouth." She laughed again. "Or Pop Rocks."

He watched her, not the fish, totally mesmerized by the fun-loving, gregarious woman inside her. "Weren't those the candy things that exploded in your stomach if you drank them with soda?"

Her eyes sparkled. "That's an urban legend."

Racking his brain for ways to keep her smiling, he said, "Want to hear a Maverick legend?"

She flipped off her cap and lay back against the rock. "Of course."

"When my sister was about six years old, my parents sent us out to find a puppy for her."

She turned her head. "I thought you said you didn't have pets."

"There was one pretty big caveat—the puppy had to be a stuffed toy. But that cost money, so we needed ingenious ways to follow Mom's edict. Without stealing. She'd tan our hides if we did that."

"With the rolling pin."

"Yup," he said, grinning. "With her white-haired-old-lady rolling pin."

Smiling back, she said, "So what did you all do?"

"Will entered a street-boxing match. He won, of course, then took his prize money to buy Lyssa a Saint Bernard big enough to ride. At the same time, Matt, who was all about mechanics and robotics, mastered one of those arcade grab machines where you use levers to pick up toys. He got three stuffed puppies."

"You guys are wonderful."

"Wait, there's more. Sebastian charmed a salesgirl into selling him a puppy with a missing eye. He got it for a quarter, then he sewed up the eye and told Lyssa that she had to take very good care of her one-eyed puppy. Then Evan, like the financial wizard that he's always been, played the stores off each other, telling the clerk that the store over there sold the same thing for a cheaper price. In the end, he price-matched them down to almost nothing."

"And you? What did you do?"

"I rode a bus to a really expensive neighborhood and shopped their thrift stores. The stuffed animals looked like they'd never been used, by kids who had way too many toys. I got them for a song." He grinned. "Lyssa ended up with a dozen stuffed animals. They were all over her bed, and she insisted on sleeping with every single one every night."

"Even the Saint Bernard?"

"He stood guard at the bottom of her bed. I think she might still have some of them."

"Thank you," Tasha said suddenly, the words seeming to fall from her lips before she could stop herself.

He turned his head to look her in the eye. "For

what?"

"For helping me see that not all men are bad. Some men, like you, are so very good."

Chapter Eighteen

The depth of emotion in Tasha's voice touched Daniel like nothing ever had. "You're so beautiful," he told her.

"You're the beautiful one."

"Tasha." He needed her to know, "I won't hurt you."

She sat up and stared into his eyes, and he swore he could see all the way into her soul. "But what if I'm the one who hurts you?"

"You won't," he promised, wanting nothing more than to lean in to kiss her. But it had to be her choice—if it wasn't, nothing would ever truly change for them.

Their first kiss had been a sudden, shocking burst of glorious heat. Their second had been a mash-up of emotions—relief, longing, desire. Daniel knew their third, and all the others that came after, could be so much more.

But only if Tasha allowed herself to want him, to open up to him, to truly be with him.

For long, excruciating moments, he waited. While she weighed the pros and cons, measured the good and the bad, fought yet another battle with herself over what she believed to be right and what she was absolutely certain was wrong.

He wanted to sway her, to show her that the two of them were all *pros* and *goods* and *rights*. But she wasn't a building that could be put together by taking careful measurements and using the right tools.

Tasha was a flesh-and-blood woman whose heart and soul had been crushed by the people she trusted most. No matter how badly he wanted to lead her toward happiness, she needed to rebuild at her own pace, in her own way.

Letting her breath go, she made her decision. His heart hammered inside his chest, and he feared she might pull away, turn from him, and close up again.

Instead, her lips brushed over his, like dragonfly wings. Soft and gentle, barely there. Teasing him with everything he wanted from her.

"More," he whispered, relief—and desperate desire—drenching every letter of the word.

With a hand cupping his cheek, she angled deeper, taking him exactly where he wanted to go. He couldn't breathe without breathing her in. He couldn't swallow without tasting her. He couldn't move without the delicious feel of her against him.

She pushed him back on the rock, leaning over him, her scent enthralling his senses, her ponytail falling over her shoulder to caress his cheek as she kissed him. Wrapping his arms around her, he held her tight. Her heat surrounded him, turning him as hard as the rock beneath them.

But her mouth was the delicacy he couldn't get enough of—and she seemed to feel the same urgency as she took him with long, delicious sweeps of her tongue, toying with him, tangling with him, consuming him with desire.

He pulled her hair free, letting it fall over them like strands of silk. He filled his hands with her, from the round firmness of her hips, pressing her hard against him, to her magical hair that had a life all its own, binding him to her.

"You're so sweet," he whispered between deep kisses that satisfied his need to taste, yet drove him to crave everything from her. "You make me lose my mind."

He'd lost it the instant he'd seen her hanging from the roof, his fear choking him, yet sensing even then how strong she was. From the moment he'd pulled her against him on that ladder and felt her lush curves, he'd wanted her.

She lit up something inside him that had never experienced such a bright and beautiful glow.

"Don't stop," she murmured, her lips on his.

He was as alive as the mountains around them, as full of joy as the squirrels chattering in the trees, as wild as the hawk flying over them.

A voice broke through. "Mommy, can I go swimming?"

Daniel expected Tasha to jump away, just as she'd pulled from his embrace with each of their two heart-melting kisses. But this time, she slid her fingers through his hair to hold him still as her lips took another sip from his. Then she laughed softly, sweetly, and moved to sit with her feet in the water just as the family appeared around the bend.

★ ★ ★

Tasha had tried yet again to do the right thing, to stop them both from taking a step that might hurt Daniel. But then he'd made her a promise that changed everything—he'd vowed he wouldn't let her hurt him.

Absolutely certain that Daniel Spencer never made a promise he couldn't keep, she finally gave in to the heat, the need, the desperate longing—and kissed him.

She'd known from their first two delicious kisses that it would be good. But she'd honestly had no idea how *amazing* good could be.

For the first time in a very long while, Tasha felt wildly free, with the sun on her head, the fish nibbling at her toes, and Daniel's taste on her lips.

"You're a naughty man," she said as he brushed his fingertips lightly over the sensitive skin of her collar-bone, even as the family of four sat on the rocks only a hundred feet away.

Putting his free hand to his chest, he teased her with a wide-eyed look. "Who, me?"

When they were like this—laughing together in the

sunshine—he almost made her feel like the last bad months had never happened. Like she was the light-hearted woman she'd been before she'd learned the truth about her family.

A woman who couldn't stop smiling as she said, "My brother and I were always outside as kids. Splashing in ice-cold streams. Climbing any tree we could get into." She waited for the pain to come from talking about her brother, but felt only the joy of their childhood instead.

Daniel's kiss—and his promise—were even more powerful than she'd realized.

"What else did the two of you do?" Daniel asked.

"We played lots of games. Our favorite was *Stratego*, that strategy game where you have military battles. He got used to winning, until one day he didn't win so easily anymore." She laughed at the memory of how stunned her brother had been once she became old enough to turn the tables. "One time we had a day out by ourselves with ice cream and hot dogs. It was wonderful. I saw this little china horse in a shop. I wanted it so bad, but I'd spent all my allowance already. Drew bought it for me." The memory was so poignant, she could remember the exact curve of her brother's smile. "I had it for years and years."

"What happened to it?"

It was so nice to finally talk freely about her brother, that when the pain hit, it was a sucker punch she didn't see coming. "It broke when I was packing up my stuff for storage before I came here."

Daniel curled his fingers around her hand. "How did it break?"

"I broke it." Just as the truth about her brother had broken her. Tears ached behind her eyes. But Daniel just kept holding her hand, a soft, soothing stroke of his thumb across the back. "I want so badly to believe in him. But how can I, after what he did? And for how long he did it? How can I forgive myself for being so blind all these years?"

Daniel didn't answer right away, until he began to speak with a pain she felt inside her own body. "You've probably figured out from talking with the guys this weekend that Evan's ex-wife was in no way worthy of him. None of us liked Whitney. She did a lot of really bad things." He stopped, staring out over the lake, then finally brought his gaze back to her. "She told unforgivable lies that almost destroyed Evan."

Tasha tried to swallow past the lump in her throat. "And here I thought you were going to tell me she actually turned out to be a nice person when you all got to know her."

He laughed without a hint of humor. "The more we knew, the more we hated her. But Evan was blind. And you know who else was blind? My mom. She defended Whitney up one side and down the other. She always found reasons for why Whitney did this or why she did that. She was our voice of acceptance. Until one day even Mom couldn't remain blind anymore."

"I'm so sorry."

"I'm not. Especially now that Evan's finally with the woman of his dreams. But my mom doesn't blame herself for not seeing through Whitney. She hasn't stopped believing in people. That's one of the things I love best about my mother—she refuses to let her faith be shaken by one truly rotten person. She still believes you have to look for the best in people until they prove you wrong." He gave Tasha's hand a tight squeeze. "Here's another miracle. Just when Evan was splitting up with his wife, his long-lost mother, who abandoned him when he was a kid, showed up, along with a brother and sister Evan never knew he had."

The trials Evan's family had been through were staggering. No wonder he was so intent on protecting Daniel. "How on earth did he deal with all that?"

"Paige. She was a rock for him, even when he stupidly tried to push her away."

Was Daniel trying to reveal something with that statement—did he think Tasha was foolish for trying to keep her distance after he'd offered her so much support?

"The other guys and I hated his birth mother for walking out on Evan when he was a kid and leaving him with his monster of a father. But Mom gave Evan's mother a chance to apologize, to make amends, and to love Evan the way she'd always loved him from afar. And I've got to say, over the last six months, having his birth mother and siblings around him has been really good for him."

"You've also forgiven his birth mom, haven't you?" Tasha asked.

Daniel held her with his gorgeous brown eyes. "You know what? I think I have. She made some really big mistakes, but she truly does love Evan." He caressed Tasha's cheek so sweetly a pang circled her heart. "Thank you for helping me see that."

"Maybe one day, I'll be able to forgive my family too," she said, her voice barely loud enough to be heard over the shrieks of laughter from the children several rocks over.

If she *did* find her brother and father through the feelers she'd put out, and if she was able to confront them, was there any chance their reckoning could lead to forgiveness?

Or would she only end up feeling more broken inside?

"I know how badly you want that," Daniel said. "Especially your brother. But if you ask me, the far more important question is—can you forgive yourself?"

She'd been staring at the water, watching the ripples, the sparkles of sunlight across the surface, when she had to bring her gaze back to his. "Like your mother forgave herself for being wrong about Evan's wife?"

"Looking for the best in people is one of the most

admirable things about my mother," Daniel said, "even if she hasn't always gotten it right."

"I'd love to be like her." *Admirable.* "And like you—able to forgive. I'm just not sure I have it in me."

"I *know* you have it in you, Tasha." Daniel's gaze, and his touch, were as gentle and sweet as only a strong man's could be.

Then he kissed her until she wanted to believe him.

Chapter Nineteen

They returned in time to take the puppies for a walk, then Daniel fed Tasha another delicious barbecue dinner. When the evening turned chilly and the puppies crawled into their crate to sleep, Daniel piled pillows and an extra comforter in front of the fire.

The flames crackled soothingly, the wine he poured making her bones melt. But it wasn't really the wine.

It was Daniel.

Their kisses by the lake had been beyond magical. But she still felt deeply conflicted about taking things any further when her life was still such a total and complete mess. How could he possibly want to get involved with a woman who came from a family of liars and con men, who had no job prospects, and who lived in a mountain shack?

"I should go," she made herself say, though it was the last thing she wanted.

"Don't go yet. I'm not done learning about you."

She felt like he knew absolutely *everything* about her by now. She'd revealed the loneliness she'd felt these last months. How hard it had been to leave her adult friends behind, the same way she'd left friends over and over again as a child. The way her father's words had ripped her in two back on that cold February day.

Daniel had helped her remember some of the good things she'd forgotten—fun, carefree times with her brother, how strong their bond had been as children. Daniel's support was also integral to helping her find the courage to get online and start looking for her brother and father. He'd made her take a hard look at whether she truly was *so* bad, *so* blind, *so* foolish—and whether giving up her own happiness was really a necessary part of making reparations to everyone her family had hurt. He'd made her question whether her sins were truly the same as her father's.

"Don't think, Tasha." Daniel obviously read her mind, recognized the panic rising close to the surface. Had he read the depth of her emotions for him too? "Just like I'm not going to think. Because if I do, I'll see that everything's going too fast for you. That you need more time to heal, to process, to trust again." He stopped, her own thoughts reflected in the fire of his gaze. "Please don't ask me to let you go tonight."

It was clear what he wanted, but he was giving her the choice, not forcing her. Neither seducing nor coercing.

More than anything else, he was asking her to be honest with him. As honest as he'd been with her. And she'd been trying so hard to keep him safe from her that she hadn't let herself admit how much she wanted him. How much she needed him.

Or how deep, how true, her feelings for him ran.

After everything they'd shared today, the thought of walking out that door tore something loose inside. Something he'd only just begun to help her stitch back together at the lake.

"I don't want you to let me go tonight."

His smile lit up the room, and in the next moment, he pulled her down, rolling her beneath him, whispering, "Are you sure?"

An answering smile bloomed inside her. "Completely sure."

He stroked the hair from her face. "It's still your choice. It will always be your choice. I will never take that away from you."

"I know you won't." She laid her palm over his. "I choose to stay." Though it felt totally unromantic, she needed him to know one more thing. "I'm on the Pill." She hadn't planned on being with anyone in the near future, but she'd kept the prescription for the other benefits, like regulating her cycle. "And I haven't been with a man for a very long while."

"There hasn't been anyone for me for a while either," he told her. "So you don't have to worry about me."

Trailing kisses across her cheek, he finally found her lips, teasing and tantalizing. He didn't rush—he savored. He whispered between each kiss—sweet, sexy, beautiful things.

"Your skin is so damn soft, you make me crazy." He angled, taking her mouth again. "I dream about you at night, how good you taste." She melted into his words. "I see your smile. I hear your laugh." He threaded his fingers through her hair. "And your tool belt drives me *wild*."

She laughed, and it felt wonderful and free. Tonight, she would forget her fears, her inhibitions. Wrapping her arms around his neck and pulling him down, all that mattered was *Daniel*. His touch, his scent, his kiss.

He rolled her on top, and she kissed him until she felt drugged with his taste. Needy for more, she slid her hands beneath his shirt to feel bare skin against her fingertips. His muscles were taut, his body hard.

Then he switched it up again, taking her beneath him, one leg between her thighs, then the other, spreading her as though she were a feast. "I want to taste you everywhere." His eyes glittered, dark and hot, but he paused to let her respond. To say no if she had to.

Or to beg if she couldn't help herself.

The choice was obvious. *"Yes, please."*

His glittering gaze on her, he pushed up her shirt slowly, baring her abdomen, bending for a kiss, then a long swipe of his tongue. Her skin quivered.

"So sweet," he whispered against her stomach, sliding the shirt still higher, trailing kisses as he worked his way up.

Her need was so intense she panted, specially when he tugged her shirt over her breasts, tracing the edge of her bra with his tongue.

She didn't wear fancy stuff anymore. But Daniel had set her sexuality free again—and now she wished she could have worn silk and lace and satin for him.

Fortunately, he didn't seem to care in the least that she wore plain cotton as he toyed with the front clasp of her bra. "So pretty." He snapped it open, pushed the shirt and bra off, then sighed his pleasure, sending a wash of tantalizing warm breath over her. "You're absolutely gorgeous. Even better than my fantasies."

She arched into his mouth on her breasts, pushing her head back into a pillow as a long, low moan slipped from her lips. She was all liquid warmth, wanting him, needing him inside her as he turned her inside out. Made her wild.

She writhed beneath him as he laved the taut tip of one breast and took the other between his fingertips, circling, teasing, pinching lightly. She gasped for breath, dragging in air.

Yesyesyes fell from her lips as easily as her moans.

When he bit lightly on her sensitive flesh, she cried out, drawing up her legs to wrap them around his waist, holding him as close as they could get without stripping their clothes off.

With his mouth still on her breast, he shifted, pressing tight between her legs.

And she was lost.

★ ★ ★

As Tasha trembled beneath him, gasping, arching, crying out, Daniel moved his hips as though he were inside her, increasing the friction of their jeans between them. She shuddered with pleasure in his arms, and he savored her gorgeous cries and moans as the waves of bliss coursed through her. There were no words for how perfect she was—the beauty of her body, the muscles that rippled beneath her sleek skin.

He'd always been in control in bed—but with Tasha, his fingers fumbled at the fastening of her jeans, jerking the zipper. He'd never made a woman come with only his mouth on her breast and his clothed body between her legs. Just as he'd known from the start, something primal blazed between them.

He'd never felt this wild need for anyone. Never thought he would find a woman who could turn his world inside out.

Not until Tasha fell into his arms. Into his life.

And he was undone.

He wanted to make this so damn good for her, so much more than sex, more than pleasure. He wanted the intimacy they'd shared at the lake when they revealed their secrets to each other. He wanted to explore all her hidden places and make her forget everything but that they belonged together.

She laid her hands on him. "I need to see you. All of you."

Going back on his haunches, he pulled her up until they faced each other, her knees between his legs. She pushed his shirt up and off.

"You are so magnificent," she said, then lowered her head to his chest and licked him.

His hands shook with the effort it took not to grab her, take her, claim her as his. He'd never known pleasure could be so damn intense, quaking through his limbs, his muscles bunched hard against the need to have her right this freaking second.

Splaying her fingers over his abdomen, she teased along his waistband, flattened her hands against his rib cage. When she palmed his erection, he lost all control, hauling her to him.

"Do you have any idea how good you feel?" he asked, his voice rough.

She rubbed her cheek against his chest. "If it's anything like how you feel against me…"

He had to kiss her again, had to taste the salt of their skin, his and hers together, before he came down beside her, laying her back so that he could gaze into her eyes. "Let me love you."

Her eyes closed at the word *love*, but she nodded. Mouthed the word *yes*.

This time he didn't allow his hands to shake as he parted her jeans and pulled them, plus her panties, past her hips and down her legs.

Gorgeous.

Slowly, he worked his way down her body, tasting every curve, every rib, the flat of her stomach, teasing her belly button. He'd never rushed through lovemaking. But he'd never wanted to linger for hours either.

Not until Tasha.

★ ★ ★

Daniel's mouth on her was an out-of-body experience. She was floating somewhere, her hands in his hair as she rocked against him, the intensity building inside.

Someone—she barely realized it was herself—made soft keening noises. *"Daniel."*

She'd never let go like this, not for anyone. A part of her had always been slightly embarrassed, worried she wouldn't be able to look her lover in the eye once the moment had passed.

But Daniel stripped away her fears. They were simply man to woman, yin to yang, lover to lover. She felt as though she knew him, as though she could say anything to him, do anything, ask anything.

And be totally accepted.

His mouth still driving her wild, he moved his fingers over her, then inside. A bolt of sizzling hot sensation burst over her, and she called out his name, her fingers fisted in his hair, her body arching, then bowing as he propelled her to the peak before pitching her off into sweet, hot oblivion.

She'd never held a man tighter.

And she'd never felt closer to anyone.

When she could finally move again, think again, she held out her arms. Reading her as though she'd opened the pages of her whole life to him, he moved up her body to hold her.

"*Please.*" She couldn't remember ever begging before. But then, no man had ever given her such pleasure, such sweetness, as though he knew her mind and her needs completely. "I need you."

When he slid his hips into the perfect place and slowly—*blissfully*—moved inside her, she felt the immensity of their bodies coming together for the first time...and yet it was as though they'd done this forever. Dancing together in perfect passion.

She'd been empty for months, lonely, aching. But as Daniel filled her, she understood how truly empty she'd been for so very long before that.

Arms wrapped around him, binding him to her, she whispered, "Don't move yet." She needed the feel of him to imprint itself inside her.

"Am I hurting you?"

"No." He was bigger than anyone she'd known, but he was Daniel—he could never hurt her. "I'm memorizing the feel of you," she confessed.

A surprised laugh burst from him a beat before he flexed inside her. She half laughed, half groaned at his sexy move. "Do that again."

When he did, she was amazed by how deliciously the slight tensing increased the friction inside her.

Laughter was soon taken over by desire and heat as she folded her legs around his waist and demanded, "More."

His movements were dizzying as he slowly, relentlessly, gave rise to the sweetest pleasure. She moaned again, parting her lips, and he raised his head from the crook of her neck to take her with a deep kiss that invaded her body, her mind.

Making her utterly, inexorably his.

★ ★ ★

Daniel had never been this close to losing control. He'd wanted a slow ride, stroking her inside just enough to keep her on edge, until she begged for more.

But Tasha undid him completely.

Unable to stop his body from taking over, pushing faster, harder, deeper, cupping her hips, he took them both on a desperate ride into the depths of pleasure. His blood pounded through him as her fingers dug into him, urging him on. Even her scent changed to something spicy and hot.

With her body gripping him tightly, her pleasure reached its peak and exploded around him, the sensations so intense she brought him straight to heaven with her.

When he finally came back to earth, their bodies were slick and hot, melded together. As though they were one. He didn't want to move, couldn't let her go.

She mumbled something unintelligible, and he

kissed her damp forehead, brushing her hair back as she said more clearly, "I'm not usually like that, so wild. I don't—"

He hushed her with a finger to her lips. "I loved every moment with you. Exactly the way you were. Carried away. Out of yourself. *Wild.* That's how I felt too." He gazed at her, wanting so much *more*. "Come to bed with me and we can be wild all over again." He waited for her to balk, his gut tensed.

"I'll only come to your bed," she said in a husky voice, "if you promise to do *that* to me again."

He gathered her close, loving how she made him laugh, how she made him shout with pleasure. "How could I not?" Then he flexed inside her, the way she'd loved, to prove his point.

He adored the moan that rose in her. He wanted to hear it over and over. Not just all night long.

Forever.

Chapter Twenty

Daniel woke Tasha again and again in the night, for sweet, drugging kisses, to touch her and make her sigh and moan and gasp with pleasure, to fill her gloriously with his body, banishing her loneliness.

But now the one night she'd given herself to break free was over. With the sun shining brightly in her eyes, Tasha was struck by stark terror, her stomach literally lifting and dropping.

Even before she'd exiled herself to the mountains, any pleasure she'd previously experienced was nothing compared to what she now felt with Daniel. He didn't believe she needed to atone for any sins—but she was stricken anew with the sense that the happiness she'd found in his arms was yet again a betrayal of the people her family had hurt.

And there was Daniel himself. He was a billionaire, for God's sake. Despite his easygoing nature, never shoving his wealth in anyone's face, he still belonged to a world she'd only read about in magazines and books.

It was so tempting to run again. The way she'd been running for months.

But running was no longer the answer. Not even from this wellspring of emotion that was bigger than anything she'd ever known.

She scrunched her eyes shut, wishing it were night again, wishing she could stay burrowed in Daniel's warm, strong body forever. But no matter how desperately she wanted that, she couldn't ignore the fact that he'd be gone soon.

The thought of Daniel returning to the Bay Area and his home-improvement empire made her heart ache, even though she understood why he couldn't stay in the mountains. There were too many employees, friends, and family counting on him.

She would cherish the memory of their blissful night forever, but the demons she battled were still too big for her to believe that she and Daniel could become anything more than mountain lovers. And friends—she wouldn't cheapen what they'd shared by denying that they were friends too.

When he was gone, she would have to push past the ache inside her to focus on finding not only any outstanding victims of her family's scams who needed financial reparations, but also on locating her brother and father. She had to be sure they never played their dirty tricks again. She hadn't saved their past victims, but she would make certain there were none in the future.

As though they could feel her pain, the puppies started to whine, their cries wending along the hallway.

She pried the covers off, but Daniel was quicker. "You stay here. I'll let them out."

"I'll come with you."

But he was kissing her cheek, her ear, her hair, her shoulder. "I have plans for you and this bed. *Lots* more." He grinned that gorgeous, wicked smile of his as he slid away from her and left the bedroom.

It was obvious when he reached Spanky, Froggy, and Darla, because their excited yipping sounded like that of ten puppies instead of three.

She glanced at her watch, the only thing she'd worn in his bed. How the heck could it be nine a.m. already? She owed him hours and hours of work on his house to pay him back for all he and his friends had done for her.

Her clothes hung over the footboard—he must have brought them in last night after putting the puppies to bed—and she pulled on everything, intending to get fresh things at her place before returning here to work. Without a toothbrush or a comb, the best she could do was to put some toothpaste on the end of her finger to rub onto her teeth, and run her fingers through her hair to get out the worst of the tangles.

Only to stop as she remembered exactly how those tangles got there. His hands in her hair, his mouth on hers, the delirious abandon as she threw her head back against the pillows while he kissed and caressed her.

Her lips felt swollen from his endless kisses. Her

whole body felt relaxed, sated. She closed her eyes and stretched, rolling her shoulders, letting her head fall back, reliving with every movement all their luscious lovemaking.

She didn't realize he'd entered the bedroom until his arms wrapped around her from behind. "You look just like you did last night, every time you came for me." He dropped kisses in her hair, the sensitive spot in the crook of her neck, making her tremble for him all over again. "Now that the puppies are settled, let's get back into bed."

"But it's already nine o'clock. I promised to work on your house with you."

"I'll show you exactly what we can work on," he whispered seductively, "right there, in that bed."

She was so languid and warm, she might have let him toss her right back under the covers. But her stomach growled. So loudly it was practically the roar of a lion.

"Hmm, sounds like I'd better feed you first." He waggled his eyebrows, so cute and absolutely too seductive. "We need to keep your strength up."

★ ★ ★

For Daniel, their night together had been flawless, dazzling. Tasha was inside him now, part of him. Even while they finished their breakfast outside on his deck, he wanted to pounce on her and have his wicked way with her in the glorious sun and the fresh air.

He could still taste her on his tongue, seducing his senses with her scent, and relished the memory of how she'd trembled against him. Even better, he understood there was no way Tasha would have allowed herself to make love to him if she hadn't felt at least an inkling of forgiveness and acceptance. Surely by now a part of her had to believe that not everything about her family's con was her fault.

All he could think as she got up to clear their plates was that no one had ever made dishwashing sexy. Until Tasha.

He was such a goner. And he couldn't have been happier about it.

"So," she said, "what can I help you with today?"

A good half-dozen naughty responses leaped to his tongue. He was still picking his favorite when she held up her hand, clearly reading his dirty mind. Probably because she had one too—he'd confirmed that last night to the best of his ability, after all.

"While wearing a tool belt," she clarified.

Oh yeah. There were of *plenty* of fun things they could do together while she had on a tool belt. In fact—

He leaned forward to tap the bill of her cap. "We need to get you a special ball cap that says *I do everything better with my tool belt on.*"

"Daniel." She pursed her lips and raised an eyebrow like a schoolmarm. The sexiest damn schoolmarm on the planet. And she was trying so hard not to smile. "We should work on your house."

Yesterday, he'd convinced her to take a little time off, but he obviously wouldn't get away with it twice. Still, even doing carpentry, he planned on getting away with plenty—teasing her until she begged, touching her on the sly, kissing her until she was delirious.

"Okay, we can get to work. But let's head up to your place, since finishing the paneling in your cabin is a two-person job and I've only got a day or two left before I need to head back to the office."

Tasha paled at his words, and though he never wanted to cause her pain, his heart gave a little kick at seeing her react to the idea of his leaving.

"I'm amazed you've been able to get away for this long." She was attempting nonchalance, but from where he stood, it seemed like she couldn't quite take in enough air.

He *hated* the thought of leaving her. Then it hit him: What if she came with him?

He'd spent his whole life looking for *perfect*, assuming that was where he'd find real happiness. Yet he'd found his greatest joy in the middle of what anyone would call a big fat mess.

A week ago he'd thought messes were to be avoided at all costs. Yet now he wanted that messiness with everything he was. Maybe the road was supposed to have bumps. Maybe working through those bumps together made you stronger.

The one thing he knew for sure was that Tasha belonged with him.

The only question was, how the heck to convince her to go back together?

Chapter Twenty-One

The fleeting time Daniel had left in Lake Tahoe played around and around in Tasha's head as they worked on her cabin's paneling.

He'd given her a taste of how wonderful they could be together. How good it was to talk, to work side by side, to play with the puppies together. Not to mention the tantalizing, sexy feelings he evoked in her.

Delicious sensations that bubbled up every time his hand brushed hers when they lifted a panel. Or when his touch lingered after he'd handed her a tool. Or when he stood so close she felt faint from the delicious heat of his body and his spicy scent.

With his shirt off, his jeans riding low on his hips, and his tanned skin covered in a sheen of sweat, he was the epitome of the sexy construction worker.

Tasha's mouth watered.

"Hold it here," he directed, and his words, especially his tone, dragged her back to last night in his sleigh bed when he'd given her the most glorious sensual commands imaginable.

As she held the panel in place against the wall, he

shifted behind her, his body sliding against her, the scent of the soap he'd used in the shower surrounding her.

He was doing it on purpose, touching her like this, the contact making her dizzy. Fifteen minutes ago, he'd kissed her until she nearly swooned like a Southern belle who'd laced her corset too tightly. Then he'd gone right back to hanging the next piece of paneling, a grin playing around the edges of his mouth.

Needing to cool off a bit—her concentration was so bad at this point she might accidentally cut off a finger—she said, "I'm just going to check the puppies."

Of course they were fine. They had plenty of water in their pen, and after they'd scarfed down some kibble, they became so energized that a wrestling match ensued among all three. Tasha was pleased that Darla had grown strong enough to hold her own with her two bulkier brothers. Even better, she was usually the winner with her quick and wily moves.

Returning to the bedroom, Tasha almost swooned—again. Daniel stood spread-eagled against the wall, hammering a piece high up. The work was seamless as he stepped back to inspect it.

The paneling be damned—he was all she saw. The play of muscles across his broad back. Lean hips in well-worn jeans. She was speechless. Dizzy with lust.

Her heart beat wildly as she crossed the room. The *clomp* of her tool belt hitting the floor should have alerted him, but he didn't turn. Part of the tease, she was sure, because he had to know how edible he looked, so much so that she was dying to take a bite out of him.

Gliding her arms around him from behind, she slid her hands along his waist. Without second-guessing herself, she unbuckled his tool belt and tossed it aside with a *thunk*. Then she popped the button of his jeans.

She'd never been this bold with a man. But Daniel gave her the courage to do the things she wanted, to say the things she'd always kept inside. With him, she forgot her natural inhibitions. Yet, in all the things they'd done last night, *this*—giving him the same pleasure he'd given her so many times in the night— hadn't been one of them. She'd been so fevered and wild, she could think of nothing else but being with him.

As he turned to face her, the need burning in his eyes made her feel powerful and wonderful and free. And happy enough to wipe out, for another few blissful moments, the turmoil of her past.

Throwing herself at him, she kissed him with all the pent-up desire he was so expert at building inside her. She ran her fingers down his rock-hard chest, over his incredible abs, down to the zipper of his jeans. He was so hard, so big, she could barely get the zipper down. Her hands shook—*all* of her shook—with the desperation to feel him, to taste him, to make love to him.

She curled her fingers around him even as she

dropped to her knees and pulled him free. She wet her lips, tingling from head to toe with need. "You really are magnificent."

"So are you," he said.

She *felt* magnificent in this moment. What they were doing wasn't coarse or crude. It was sexy. It was honest.

And it was beautiful.

"Just one more thing." He tossed her ball cap aside and pulled the elastic from her hair, letting the tresses float over her shoulders.

She couldn't wait a moment longer, didn't give herself time to worry she might be bad at it. She could never be bad at something she wanted this much.

There was the pleasure of his taste, the decadent feel of him against her tongue, and the lovely knowledge of her effect on him. His groans were husky, the words falling from his lips sweet and filthy, his legs shaking as though he could barely stand.

He shoved his fingers through her hair and held her as his hips took over the rhythm. She reveled in his surrender as much as his taste.

Then he hauled her up, anchoring her legs around his waist. "I love what you're doing. But I need more. I need *you*." He stalked with her out to the living room, where her air mattress lay in the corner.

"Wait, we can't do it there." She almost laughed at her practical side rearing itself *now*, of all times. "It'll burst."

"If it does, I'll get you a new one." Then he grinned, utterly confident that he had her right where he wanted her. And right where she wanted to be. "Or you can sleep in my bed from now on."

They'd never get up if they slept in his sleigh bed. They almost hadn't this morning. He dropped hot little kisses on her mouth, her cheeks, her nose, her eyes, and the idea blossomed that maybe, oh yes, positively, staying in bed all day with Daniel wasn't a bad idea at all.

He knelt, letting her fall back before he came down on top of her, her legs still wrapped around him. "See, it didn't burst."

"Yet," she said, tossing out her challenge with a laugh. She'd never known making love could be so much fun. But this was Daniel and everything about him was incredible.

"Do you have any idea what that tool belt and those shorts of yours have been doing to me all morning?" He slid his fingers into the fabric, cupping her hips. "It was like you didn't have anything else on."

She could only moan in response as he touched her in all the right places.

"I want to take you so slowly," he whispered, "that you're panting."

She wound her arms around his neck and pulled him down, her lips on his. "I'd rather have you really fast and hard."

"We'll do both." He kissed her into agreement,

then came close to ripping her shorts in his haste to get her naked, settling for letting them dangle from one leg.

Then, with little more than shoving his jeans over his hips, he entered her.

Fast.

Hard.

Perfect.

She gasped as he filled every bit of her, even the part of her heart she swore had emptied itself out forever that horrible day back in February.

Then he moved ever so slowly, and she gripped his shoulders, the solid feel of him beneath her fingers keeping her from floating away. It was the stuff of fantasies, the way things felt when you closed your eyes and imagined. Only, this was real.

He was real.

"I think...I think..." What was she thinking? Oh God, she couldn't think at all. "I need to be on top." She wanted to stretch her arms over her head and ride him.

"I need you there too." He rolled with her, and they fell off the bed onto the floor, laughing.

But even laughing with him was sexy, and soon her eyes were closing as he found just the right spot inside.

"God, yes," he growled, "you feel good."

Every touch, every kiss, every taste and lick, everything they did was completely delicious. His fingers only made it better as he yanked off her shirt and bra and splayed his hands over her breasts, shooting jolts of pleasure straight down to her center.

She closed her eyes as she gathered her hair in her hands and curled her arms over her head, her body quivering with every slip-slide over that wonderful spot inside her.

"Look at you." She heard the reverence in his voice. "Look at *us*."

She opened her eyes to find him watching the movement of her body as he filled her on every downstroke and revealed his majesty as she climbed up.

Nothing had ever been more beautiful. Nothing had ever felt so sweet. So good. So right.

He moved his hand between her thighs, and she gave herself over to sensation. To *Daniel*. Her breath hitched, her legs quaked, and everything inside her started to shake, contract.

She felt the build, the rush of sensation to her center, and then finally, the explosion. She cried out, and his hands moved to her hips, helping, grinding her against him—stealing her breath and her heart and her soul as together they shot straight to the sky, to the stars, to heaven.

Chapter Twenty-Two

"Come back with me."

Daniel and Tasha lay curled around each other on her bed. She felt so warm and sweet against him that he couldn't keep the request inside a moment longer.

"Come back with you?" She blinked at him as though he'd just escaped from the nuthouse.

It was too soon, and he was adding one more layer of complication to her life, but he couldn't stand the thought of leaving her behind. "I want to spend more time with you, and my next trip to Tahoe is way too long to wait." He stroked her arm, to calm her...and himself. "You can stay with me, if you want. Or you can get a hotel room, stay with a friend, even find an apartment. I just want you close. I want to see you every day like we do now. I want you to meet the guys' wives and girlfriends, brothers, sisters, mothers." He paused, wondering how hard to push. But he was already pushing so hard that he might as well go for broke. "I know my parents would love to meet you."

The silence beat against his eardrums, her body so still he didn't think she was even breathing.

Then finally, she said in a soft voice, "I want to say yes." His heart leaped with joy, practically doing a jig around the room. "But I don't know exactly where I'm going to be for a while."

"Why?" The mere thought of losing her *killed* him. "Aren't you planning to stay here in the cabin?"

"I was, but after I told you about my family, I realized I need to find my brother and father. I have to confront them. I have to know their criminal career is truly over. I want to believe my father learned something from this final scam—that losing me hurt enough to make him stop. But I won't know for sure until I see him. Until I talk with him again—this time without the shock of realizing my perfect family life had been a big fat lie. Does that make sense?"

"Of course it does." He was so proud of her for taking such a difficult step.

She breathed in deeply, then let it go on a long sigh. "I should have looked for them before now. You must think I'm a coward, hiding up here in the mountains for so long, and only putting out the first feelers online a couple of days ago."

He cupped her face, rubbing his nose against hers, offering all his comfort. "You're sexy and funny and smart and desirable and capable and honorable and the greatest thing since sliced bread. But never a coward. It was only natural to take some time to process how your family betrayed *you*. You can't beat yourself up for needing that, Tasha."

"I wish I'd gotten to this point faster." Frustration ground in her voice. "I desperately want to make sure things are right for everyone who got hurt in the cons. I want them to have justice." She scrunched her eyes shut. "And I need to see my brother and father again. Not only to hold them accountable for their actions, but to ask them *why*. Even if I can't understand, I need to know."

Given everything she'd said, he hoped she'd be pleased with what he'd already done. "The day you told me everything"—the day she'd begun to trust him—"I hired an investigator to search for any other victims of your father's schemes."

She clutched him fiercely, her gaze avid. "What have you found out?"

"The feds have done a lot, but my guy is continuing to follow the money trail."

"Which means he hasn't found anyone."

"Not yet. But we already know most of the capital was returned. My guy has learned a few things." Daniel had talked to his investigator while Tasha took the puppies for a quick walk this morning. "It turns out that while the feds already had an eye on the resort, it wasn't until they found a wire transfer to your web design company that they started hitting the venture hard, because the name Summerfield had come up in connection with previous scams."

"So you're saying that in a way, I was the one who got my father caught."

"Roundabout, yes."

His heart throbbed with the aftereffects of an adrenaline rush as he waited for her response. He'd been worried about her reaction, that it would only heap more guilt on her. Yet he had no right to keep the truth from her.

Finally, she raised her clear blue gaze to his. "If I blame myself for not seeing the truth and somehow putting an end to the scam, then it doesn't make sense to blame myself because the money he paid me is what led the investigators to him, does it?"

Relief whooshed through him. "That's pretty much what I was thinking."

"Thank you for telling me."

"I should have told you earlier. And I probably should have let you know about the investigator before I called him."

"You don't want me to beat myself up for needing time to process. And I don't want you to beat yourself up for being a take-charge kind of guy." She nestled closer, and the feel of her was like finding total acceptance. "It's who you are. You do what you think is right and ask questions later." She paused for a second. "Is your investigator looking for my brother and father too?"

He shook his head. "I couldn't take things that far without your permission."

"Please help me find them, Daniel."

He stroked the hair from her face, trailing a finger

down her cheek. "Anything for you."

With all his heart, he held her tight. Yet the question weighed heavily between them.

She hadn't said whether or not she'd come home with him.

★ ★ ★

Their time together rewound through Tasha's brain. They'd laughed. They'd made glorious, sexy love. They'd peeled away layers of the past, layers of emotion. She'd never shared so much of herself with a man and now she knew why—sharing her body was nowhere near as intimate as sharing her thoughts, her feelings, her fears. She'd even told him about Eric. She had no more secrets.

She adored the Mavericks, and she wanted so badly to meet all the other people who loved Daniel. After hearing his stories, she'd practically fallen in love with his family herself.

But she'd made such huge mistakes in the past. She'd trusted when she shouldn't have. She'd seen only the good in people until the bad had been shoved down her throat.

How was she supposed to know?

Really know?

His arm tight around her, he drew her up until she tilted her head to look at him, his lips achingly close. "I didn't ask you to come with me to pressure you. I needed you to know what I've been thinking. Just because I'm there already doesn't mean I expect you to feel the same." His beautiful smile made her heart flutter when he added, "Yet."

His confidence, his certainty—they were two of the things she loved about him. He always knew what he wanted and never gave up, going for his dreams with integrity, without screwing people over.

Daniel had taught her so many things in the past few days. After three long months of darkness, he'd shown her how to see the bright side again.

With his heartwarming stories about his mom, dad, sister, and the Mavericks, he'd proven that even if there was pain and struggle, family could still be loyal and trustworthy, that dishonesty wasn't the norm.

He'd taught her what bravery felt like. What confidence and certainty could achieve in the face of the worst odds, as long as you never gave up, never stopped going for your dreams with integrity, never stopped being honest.

If she didn't take this risk, she might never know how good it could be between them.

If she didn't make the choice to trust him, she might never find the courage to trust at all.

And if she didn't forgive herself for being blind to her father's and brother's faults, she might never live a whole and happy life.

Before her was an ocean of indecision, a mountain of fears, a continent of risk.

But there was also laughter. Trust. Sinfully sweet

heat.

And Daniel.

Every cell of her body, and every piece of her heart, told her he was worth it.

"I want to go with you."

"Are you sure?" He faltered as if afraid to believe it was true. "Even if you don't know exactly where the search for your family will lead?"

He already felt like her family. He felt like *home*. "I'm sure."

Taking her mouth, he kissed her so deeply she felt all the love inside him. All the joy. He locked his lips to hers until neither of them could breathe, backing off only enough to frame her face in his hands.

"I love you, Tasha Summerfield. I want you in my home. I want you in my life. Wherever you are, that's where I want to be."

She swallowed, blinked, moisture blurring her eyes. Then she gave him—and herself—something she'd never thought she could offer again.

"I love you too. You've helped me see that I don't need to keep punishing myself forever—and you've supported me every step of the way as I've emerged from my cocoon. I want to live again, Daniel. With *you*."

★ ★ ★

He kissed her with every ounce of the love overflowing his heart, gathering her tightly to him, devouring her lips with all the feeling bursting out of him. When he couldn't breathe anymore for want of her, when she pushed back to cup his face, peppering kisses on his mouth, his cheeks, his eyelids, he whispered, "I need to make love to you." They'd been making love all along, but this was the first loving after those momentous words.

Wrapping her arms around his neck, her body pressed hard against him, she gave him exactly what he needed. "Yes, Daniel, make love to me. Never stop."

He savored her words, the overwhelming emotions, and the bounty of her body, kissing his way down her throat to the pearled tips of her breasts. She arched, moaned, the sound rippling through him. He drank in her desire, relished the quake of her body and the sweet love words she cried out for him.

"Take me, Daniel. Take everything I am."

"I love you, Tasha. So damned much." Unable to wait another second to become one with her, holding her hips, he plunged inside her, so deeply he was sure their souls touched. "You'll never be alone again, I swear."

She cried out his name, and he took them both on a relentless ride to pleasure, to nirvana. They became one body, one mind, falling into bliss together, holding tight to each other.

He held her until his heart slowed, savoring the softness of her skin against him, the scent of her hair, the aroma of their loving. Her breathing leveled out into the gentle rhythm of sleep. He ached with the thought of moving her, waking her. This was too good to let go.

He'd fallen for her. Completely, irrevocably, wildly in love.

Tasha wasn't perfect, no more than he was. Perfect didn't exist, but real and good and loving and loyal did. She was beautiful, sensual, resourceful, and caring, but she also had real emotions, real fears, a real past. And just like a Maverick, she could move beyond the baggage.

All that meant it was long past time for him to move past his own baggage too. He needed to call his mother, to talk with her openly and honestly, to find out just what the heck, if anything, had happened between her and his father. He'd gone back and forth about telling the Mavericks, but in the end, he realized his whole dilemma had been nothing more than an excuse not to talk about it with the person he needed to: his mom. And while he was being totally honest, he hadn't mentioned his fears to Tasha, not only because he didn't want to burden her, but also because he'd been afraid to risk his heart for her that last little bit.

But Tasha's love had changed him. She made him brave enough to reach out. Her love had shown him he could forgive even Evan's mother for abandoning him. Her love gave him the strength he needed.

Easing away from Tasha's body, Daniel pulled the blankets over her. After pulling on his pants and shirt, he carried his shoes out to the front porch, putting them on before he fished his phone out of his pocket.

His mother answered with, "Hello," on the second ring.

Her greeting was another sign of that weirdness he'd been sensing. She had caller ID and she usually answered with an endearment.

He knew where he needed to begin. "I've finally found her, Mom. The woman I'm meant to be with."

"Oh honey." Emotion quavered in his mom's voice.

"Her life's a mess, and I don't care. I always thought I was looking for perfect, for what you and Dad have, but Tasha makes me see how important it is to wade into the mess right along with her. To be there for her in any way she needs me." He dropped his voice, closing his eyes to savor the words, the emotion. "I love her, Mom. And I need to help her heal her heart over things she's not truly responsible for. To help her stop blaming herself." He told her briefly about Tasha's father and brother, about the scams they'd pulled.

"Sweetheart. I'm so sorry for everything she's gone through. But you'll help her see that she's not to blame. It just takes patience and time. And she'll understand eventually. As long as she has the man who loves her right beside her." His mother sucked in a breath, and then she sniffled.

She was always emotional for her kids, hurting when they hurt, joyful when they found joy. But he knew this was different, that she was crying over whatever had been bothering her for days now.

He wasn't afraid of hearing it anymore. Tasha had shown him there were no bumps that couldn't be faced if you faced them with someone you loved.

Propping his elbows on his knees, he concentrated on his mother. "Is there something you haven't told me, Mom? About you and Dad, I mean. I keep getting this sense…"

He heard her breathing, then finally she said in a low voice, "One of the hardest things to do is to stop blaming yourself." After another deep breath, she swallowed audibly. "I still haven't completely forgiven myself for what happened in the past."

He thought of all the things someone could feel guilty about, certain that none of them could possibly be anything his mother was capable of. But he'd asked, and he was obliged to hear, no matter the cost. Just as he would do for Tasha.

"I'm listening, Mom. It's okay. I'll never judge you."

After two quick but shaky breaths, she said, "I was pregnant with you before your father and I got married."

Was *that* what she was worried about? Because it was no big deal. Lots of people got pregnant first, then married later. Even back in the eighties. There was no shame in that.

But before he could say this, she spoke again. "I

didn't tell your father. In fact, I broke up with him and didn't even let him know the real reason why."

Now *that* shocked the breath right out of him. His mother had always talked about openness and honesty. She'd kept something that major from his father?

Still, he'd asked. And he'd sworn not to judge. "It's okay, Mom." Maybe he was saying it to himself too.

As though she hadn't heard him, she said, "I just couldn't change Bob's life that way. We didn't have any money. And we were so young. My mother wanted me to give you away. She was so angry. She had all these hopes and dreams. That I'd go to college. That I'd get out of the neighborhood. She said I could never do that if I had a baby. But I wanted you, Daniel. I could never give you away. I just thought I had to make it on my own. So that Bob could make it out without me. So that he could be the one to go to college, to get out of that horrible neighborhood, to make something of himself, to have a chance at a better life."

Though he struggled not to reveal it, Daniel reeled at her confession; how could he not? His mom had left his father. Daniel had always thought they were perfect right from the start—yet she'd doubted his father's love, so much that she'd kept her pregnancy a huge secret from him.

"What happened?" He knew—they'd stayed to-gether, of course—but now he needed to understand not only how, but *why*. Just as Tasha needed to understand her family.

"Your father never could take no for an answer." His mother's laugh was soft and heartfelt. "He kept showing up, kept asking me why, if there was someone else, if I'd stopped loving him. I swear he plain wore me down until I told him the truth." She laughed again, this time with the hint of tears. "Saying it that way doesn't do your father justice. He showed me so much love that he broke through all my fear and resistance, straight to my heart. He helped me grow strong. He didn't have to insist we get married. He simply made me believe we could do anything as long as we were together."

That sounded exactly like his father, like the man Daniel had always respected and loved. He just couldn't believe his *mom* had been the one to give up.

Daniel thought of Tasha once more. She thought she was weak, and yet she was so strong, finding the courage to reveal her past, not just to him, but to the Mavericks. She'd found the courage to search for her father, her brother. Compared to the things Tasha had been through, Daniel's life had been easy. Because of the love of his parents. Because they believed in him. Because they'd never given up on him.

But maybe you couldn't learn how to give that kind of love and unconditional acceptance without hitting some hard bumps of your own. Maybe it was the bumps that taught you what was worth fighting for. And maybe it was surviving the worst of those bumps that made a person truly special.

Like Tasha.

Like his dad.

Like the mother he loved, respected, and cherished.

"I'm so glad you said yes to Dad."

"It wasn't all roses after that, sweetheart. I wish it had been. My parents stopped speaking to me. My mom said if I was going to be an idiot, she was washing her hands of me."

He'd never known his grandparents on either side, but he'd always thought it was because they'd died when he was only a toddler, not because his mom's parents had disowned her. His dad's father had died before Daniel was even born, his mother passing maybe a year afterward.

"I'm so sorry your mother didn't support you."

"Thank you, honey." But his mother's story didn't end there. "The pregnancy wasn't as easy as I'd thought it would be. I worried every second of every day. The last couple of months, I had to go on bed rest or I might have lost you. And I've always felt it was my fault because I worried myself sick. We didn't even have my income then. It was so hard on your father. He was working two jobs, sometimes three, just to make ends meet."

"Mom." Daniel wished now he'd asked these questions when he could see her, put his arms around her, tell her how much he loved her, no matter what. "It wasn't your fault."

"That's what your father always said. But I kept hearing my mother's voice in my head. And I kept thinking that if I'd done things differently, then maybe it wouldn't all be so difficult, so terrifying. After you were born, your father was the one who kept reminding me that if things hadn't happened just as they did, we wouldn't have you. That you might have been someone completely different. And I love you so much exactly the way you are."

He felt her love. He always had. He'd just always believed that his parents had taken events in their stride. That they had each other and there were never any questions, never any secrets. No big bumps that might have destroyed them.

"Later," she said, "when things were a little better, when both of us knew we had to have a bigger family, I was pregnant a couple of times. But I lost those babies. And it felt like punishment for running away from your father, for not trusting him enough to know he'd take care of us. Like I'd only ever have that one chance. Only with you."

"Mom, please. You can't blame yourself for the miscarriages." But it did explain why his mother had steadfastly stood by Whitney during all three of hers, why she'd felt so much sympathy. Until Whitney's terrible lies had come out. "And then you had Lyssa."

"I know it's probably hard for you to understand how the mind works sometimes. But everything was so different with Lyssa. We'd waited so long for her to come along. And I felt guilty about that too, as if somehow I'd betrayed you by feeling so much better about that pregnancy."

"Mom," he said, determined to make her see, "you're *way* too hard on yourself. Remember what I said about Tasha, about her family? She blames herself, but all those things were beyond her control. It's the same for you. You got pregnant out of wedlock and you did the best you could to deal with it. With me. You didn't do anything terrible."

In fact, she'd been admirable. She'd always been admirable. Just like Tasha, who thought of the misery of her father's victims, who worried that her brother had been sucked into something he didn't want, who blamed herself instead of the true culprits.

"Mom, you have to stop blaming yourself."

His mother sighed as if her burden were as heavy now as it had been back then. "Your father has said the same thing for years. And truly, Bob was the one who helped me look on the bright side again. Without him, I don't think I could have done it. But honestly, I thought I'd put it all behind me. But then when you were telling me about your quandary over Tasha, I realized I'd given you false expectations. That you believed everything had to be perfect. That the slightest mess meant nothing could work out. That love was no good if it wasn't smooth sailing. But no relationship is smooth sailing all the time. The only thing that matters is that your father never gave up on me—and he showed me I didn't have to give up on myself, or on us either. In the end, that's the most important thing of all. It's the lesson I wish I'd taught you."

"It *is* the lesson I've learned. I love you. I love Dad. You're both the greatest parents, with or without bumps along the way. And I'm not giving up on Tasha. Not ever. *You* taught me that, Mom. You and Dad. And you've also helped me see that no matter what, I can't live without her."

"Sweetheart, I love you so much." His mom was openly crying now. "I hope you'll forgive me for not telling you sooner."

"There's nothing to forgive, Mom. I love you and Dad exactly the way you are."

He wanted Tasha to forgive herself for what happened with her family, to accept that not everything had been her fault. The same was true for his mother, who had heaped guilt on herself all this time.

Daniel's father had helped her move past it. And he finally understood what he should have known all along: That was what true love was all about—not the absence of bumps, but how those bumps brought you closer together.

Now he just had to prove the same thing to Tasha.

Chapter Twenty-Three

I love you.

Tasha couldn't believe he'd said it. She couldn't believe she had too.

It was terrifying. But at the same time, it felt so right.

It absolutely *had* to be right. She couldn't make another mistake.

Daniel hadn't wasted any time taking her home with him to San Francisco. It seemed to have suddenly become his mission—to bring her into his work, into his life, to take her out of the mountains. And she would go anywhere he asked.

Yet during the four-hour drive, he'd seemed a bit pensive. Not like he was rethinking his declaration, but…something. She couldn't put her finger on exactly what. But the words and the feelings were so new between them—and leaving the mountains after a three-month, self-imposed exile was such a huge step— that she didn't quite know how to ask him whether anything was wrong. She couldn't seem to quiet her nerves. Still, she truly believed things would get easier.

Because being with Daniel was nothing short of miraculous.

They made two quick pit stops for the puppies, who traveled extremely well, especially when Tasha leaned back between the seats to talk to them through the bars of their crate. Once across the Bay Bridge, they soon arrived at Daniel's renovated apartment building near Nob Hill, with its magnificent view of the Bay and Alcatraz. When the sun set, the city lights would be spectacular.

Daniel carried the puppies in the crate, and they took the express elevator to the penthouse, a luxury top-floor apartment straight out of a James Bond movie.

"It's so beautiful, Daniel." Even though *beautiful* felt like such a paltry word for this mind-blowing home.

The entry opened directly onto a living room with floor-to-ceiling windows overlooking sparkling blue waters, sailboats, Alcatraz, city streets, and even the Marin side of the Golden Gate Bridge. Brown leather furniture matched the hardwood floors and rosewood coffee and end tables. A monstrous TV hung on the wall opposite a massive fireplace, surrounded by wood shelves filled with books, statues, porcelain, and artwork. She didn't know the artists, but it was all so tasteful it had to be hugely expensive. And were those two Ming vases in a display niche above the TV?

Daniel set the crate down just inside the entry hall

and bent to open the door.

Tasha dashed over. "You can't let the puppies out. They'll cause complete and total havoc. Their nails will scratch the floors. They'll knock over your statues and pee on your priceless carpets." Heck, she was so worried about ruining something herself that she shoved her hands in her pockets so she didn't accidentally destroy a thousand-year-old piece of art.

"The puppies will be fine," Daniel replied, utterly unconcerned about three furballs running amok. But when the still sleepy dogs seemed content to stay in the crate, he closed the door. "Let me show you my home." He took her hand.

"Did you do this shelving and inlay yourself?"

"I like working in wood, so I did the bookcases and the fireplace."

"Are those andirons something Charlie Ballard made?"

"They are." He gave her a pleased smile. "How did you know?"

"I looked her up on the Internet. Her work is very distinctive. So emotional."

"She'd love to hear you say that. When she was up here one time for dinner, she claimed the hearth needed something special."

He guided her through the dining room, which had oriental scrollwork on the table, chairs, and sideboard, then into a kitchen equipped with every utility imaginable. Copper pots and pans were slung on a rack hanging from the ceiling next to a gas range with both a griddle and a grill. Marble counters hosted the coffee maker, espresso machine, juicer, blender, mixer—the gadgets went on and on. A double oven, microwave, two sinks—just so you didn't have to move too far to fill a pan—even a wine cooler. The fridge was massive, with two top doors and a double bottom freezer.

"This is amazing." She loved to cook—in a real kitchen, not on a barbecue grill like Daniel—but had never dreamed of having access to a kitchen this fabulous.

"While you were letting the puppies out on the drive," he said, "I had my grocery service deliver something for us to cook tonight." He opened the fridge, which was large enough to climb into, revealing the ingredients for a gourmet salmon dinner.

After carrying a bowl of fresh water back for the puppies, he led her down a hallway, past a powder room and on to two extra rooms he used as a guest bedroom and his home office, the centerpiece of that room being a huge rolltop desk.

The furniture was gorgeously crafted, and yet again, she had a feeling Daniel was instrumental in their design, if not the actual building. The computer console looked like mission control at NASA. At the end of the hall, a door led to a workout room with weights and every mechanical gym device, from rowing machine to bike to treadmill, plus a mounted TV in the corner.

Through another door, she thought she'd find his bedroom, but instead, a wrought-iron spiral staircase led to the roof, where there was a huge enclosed rooftop garden resplendent with flowering bushes and potted plants.

She was totally overwhelmed.

The entire city was visible through the surrounding glass, from Grace Cathedral to the Mark Hopkins, the Fairmont, and the Pacific Club, then all the way down to the Transamerica Building, and out to the Golden Gate and the Bay. Central to the garden lay a lap pool, Jacuzzi, and a built-in outdoor kitchen with barbecue and smoker. Daniel pressed a button and the glass canopy opened, letting the warm sun stream down on them since the famed San Francisco fog hadn't yet rolled in.

Leading her to the opposite side of the pool, he opened the door to another spiral staircase heading back down. At the bottom they stepped into a huge bathroom with a whirlpool tub, tiled shower with four heads, and even a sauna.

Finally, he pulled her into his master bedroom, where a duplicate of his sleigh bed in Tahoe occupied one wall facing a fireplace.

"So tell me," he said as he drew her closer, "do you want the sleigh bed, the guest room, the Fairmont Hotel, or do you want to call a friend?"

Her body heated against his, but her mind was still trying to process the opulence. The way he lived had stricken her speechless before they'd even come out on the roof. She knew he was rich—he owned a home-improvement empire, for God's sake—but he drove a truck and wore old jeans and barbecued like any other guy. Only, the reality of Daniel's home was beyond anything she'd ever imagined. The kitchen was a cook's dream, she could live in the master bathroom, and the rooftop garden was a fantasy come true.

She wasn't sure she could live up to it, or the expectations of the man who commanded it. But this was who Daniel was—and she couldn't bear the thought of leaving him, no matter how intimidating his lifestyle might be. No matter how much money he had, no matter how big his homes or how deep his bank account, he was still the strong yet gentle man who had saved her from falling off her roof—then loved her even when she was certain she didn't deserve it.

"Sleigh bed," she whispered, feeling oddly shy as she spoke her choice aloud.

He cupped her face in his hands. "Thank the Lord," he said a beat before he took her lips in a long, sweet kiss that melted her bones, forcing her to grab his arms to hold herself up.

She lost herself in his kiss, forgot about the pool and the Jacuzzi and the sauna and the other luxuries. Daniel was all that mattered. Not his lifestyle, not his money.

Playing his fingers through her hair, he said softly, "During the drive here, all I could think about was getting you into bed."

She needed him too, needed his lovemaking to help her erase the doubts that had gripped her from the moment she'd walked through his home. She had a fleeting thought for the puppies, but they had water and they'd be fine. She needed Daniel. And he needed her.

"In the bed," she said. "On the carpet. On the sofa. In the Jacuzzi. I don't care where we make love to each other, Daniel, just as long as I'm with you."

★ ★ ★

She was all he desired. As her scent had wrapped around him in the cab of the truck, as she'd talked to him and filled his head with her voice, all he'd craved was seeing her in his home. All he'd dreamed of was this—Tasha begging him to take her.

He picked her up in his arms as if he were carrying her over the threshold. "We'll christen this bed first. Just like we christened the one in the cabin."

He'd never brought a woman here. Hotel rooms were anonymous, with fewer expectations. But this time *he* was the one with expectations. With hopes and dreams, ones he believed she shared.

During the drive, he'd wanted to tell her about his conversation with his mother, but he'd sensed Tasha was nervous and didn't want to add to her tension. Now that she was here, in his home, he wanted to revel in having her in his bed.

Afterward, once she was lying sated and relaxed in his arms, he'd tell her what his mom had gone through, and how much both she and Tasha had taught him.

He had her naked in one minute and himself in the next, then he dived on her, skin to skin. "You feel so damn good." She was smooth lines and curves, sweet scents and tastes, from her lips to her neck to her breasts, and all the way down. He covered her with kisses from her throat to her navel. Then he delved deep.

She gasped when he put his tongue to her, followed by a long moan, and a whispered, *"Daniel."*

He blew a warm breath over her. She quivered in reaction, and her fingers flexed, reaching for his hair, trying to pull him closer.

"Don't tease," she begged. "I can't wait."

But tease he did until she was like ice cream melting against his tongue. He couldn't get enough of her taste, kept her riding the edge for long, delicious minutes. Until he lifted his head, just long enough to say, "Come for me, Tasha," and he gave her what she needed, right on the mark, with his mouth and his fingers, inside and out.

She called his name, bucking against him, panting, gasping, crying out. Then she laughed, a blissfully happy sound as she fell back against the pillow, her body still quaking with aftershocks.

"Now," she said, her voice hoarse from crying out

her pleasure. "I need you now."

"After you come for me again," he told her. "Two more times. No, five more."

But he hadn't counted on the strength or the passion of her intent as she climbed on top of him. "I want to make *you* come now, the same way." She gazed at him as she slowly wrapped her hand around him. "I want to feel like you're mine. Like no one else can do this to you."

"Only you can," he vowed. "Don't you know what you do to me? Don't you know how beautiful, how wonderful, you are?"

Joy flashed through her eyes, but pain still lingered there too. Pain he would do absolutely anything to banish.

"Take me, Tasha. All of me. Any way you'll have me, I'm yours."

She ran slow, heated kisses over his face, his shoulders, his chest, then finally took him in her mouth, the long slow slide of her lips and tongue down, then back up, tearing a groan from him. His hips lifted, and she took him even deeper, teasing him with her tongue.

It was glorious. It was wild. His body trembled in reaction, his hands curled in the bed sheets, his legs quivering with the strain of holding back as she blew every circuit in his brain. Teasing him the way he'd teased her, she made him ride the blade's edge, then pulled him back without letting him jump into oblivion.

Until she whispered, *"Now."*

And he gave himself up completely to the only woman he'd ever love.

Chapter Twenty-Four

Tasha reveled in the feel of Daniel, in the words falling from his lips, in his scent, in his taste as he gave himself up to climax. Then he hauled her across his body, resting with his face buried in the crook of her neck.

"What you do to me," he whispered, his breath warm against her skin.

She'd felt every second of what she'd done to him. And it was more delicious and magnificent than anything else in her life. Ever.

It was more than sex. It was even more than love-making. It was Daniel letting go completely. For *her*.

It felt so good to drift in lazy, heavenly languor, her eyes closed, knee bent, foot between his spread legs, their fingers laced together. The sheet thrown aside, they were naked, skin against skin, deliciously sweaty.

It was sublime, like nothing she'd ever known. There was an ease to being with him she hadn't thought possible. She could have lain there forever.

Until his phone rang.

She wanted to beg him not to answer it, but she wasn't the only person in his life. What if his mother or one of his brothers was on the other end of that line? What if they needed his help?

He slid from the sheets to get his phone, and the frown on his face as he read the caller ID made Tasha's heart turn over.

"Is it your family?" she asked.

"No." He put the cell to his ear, answered, listened. Then he hit the mute button, holding the phone a long moment, looking at her. There was something in that gaze, his sweet, gentle eyes. "It's yours." He said it so softly she couldn't quite process what he meant until he added, "It's your brother. My investigator found him and gave him my number."

Tasha sat bolt upright, pulling the sheets around her, as though they could provide some sort of shield around her heart.

"Do you want to talk to him?"

Her chest squeezed tight, her stomach twisting as she said, "Yes."

Daniel's frown etched deeper. He sat on the bed right beside her, his warmth surrounding her. "I'm right here. I won't leave you." Then he handed over his phone.

"Hello." Her greeting didn't sound quite right, too scratchy and hoarse, too pained.

"Tash, it's Drew."

She knew his voice like it was her own. "I've missed you." Regardless of what her brother had done, she'd missed him like she would have missed a limb.

"I've missed you too." Drew gulped air. "It's Dad. He's had a heart attack."

"A heart attack?" Even after the anger and pain and betrayal, her heart plunged to her stomach, slamming so hard she doubled over. "Is he dead?" Her heart was screaming, *No, no, no.*

Before her brother could answer, Daniel's arms wrapped around her, like a cocoon protecting her as she cried soundless tears that felt like petals on her face. She collapsed into his embrace, his comfort as immense as the moon and stars.

"He's in the hospital. We're in LA. I need you to come, Tash. The old man wouldn't say it, but I know he wants you here."

She didn't have to think about it, especially with Daniel's arms around her, his body rocking hers. "I'll be there as soon as I can book a flight." There was no question but that she would go to her father, despite everything he'd done. Drew needed her too. "Text which hospital and the room number and any other information to this phone. I'll call you as soon as I know when I'll be there."

"Okay. Love you, Tash."

"Love you too." The automatic words came unbidden, as natural as they had been once upon a time.

"I have to go to Los Angeles," she told Daniel as soon as the phone went dark. "I have to book a flight."

"We'll fly down on my jet." He cupped her face in his powerful, gentle hands and tenderly wiped her tear-streaked cheek. "My pilot can get us out within an hour."

She was too grateful to be intimidated by the fact that he owned a jet. And so glad she didn't have to go alone. Her back-and-forth emails hadn't found her family, but Daniel, with all his resources—and most especially his love—had accomplished the impossible for her.

But then she realized, "The puppies. We can't leave them. You should stay here with them."

"No," he replied, the one short word fierce. "I want to be there for you. And I've got an easy solution— we'll take the puppies to Matt in Morgan Hill. It will be faster to drive there and have my pilot meet us in San Martin. There's a small airport he can fly into."

Suddenly overwhelmed by everything that had happened in the last few days, by everything this gorgeous, wonderful man had done for her, she could only nod, unable to speak. Unable to adequately express her emotions, her gratitude.

Daniel held her still. "Look at me," he whispered. "Everything will be okay." He kissed her with a sweet, wondrous brush of his lips across hers. "I'm here."

With a muffled cry, she threw her arms around his neck.

How could she possibly deserve this man?

★ ★ ★

Despite everything her family had done, it was obvious

Tasha would have crossed mountain ranges through deep snow to get to her father's side.

She had a purity of love and spirit. She was loyal. Her caring had no limits.

Daniel had never had a doubt that she was Maverick material, and her reactions today only solidified that knowledge. This was what she needed—to find her family. After his phone call with his mom, he'd been more determined than ever to help Tasha forgive herself, even if in his own heart, he didn't believe she'd done anything wrong.

Just as his mom had done nothing wrong. She'd been young and scared and had handled the crisis the best she could. Daniel was the one who'd turned their love story into one of perfection instead of something real.

At last, he'd learned that *real* was so much better.

Real was loving Tasha. Real was helping her through this difficult reunion, helping her deal with her past. Helping her find forgiveness for both herself and her family.

With rush hour over, they made it to Matt's house in an hour and a half. In the backseat of the truck, the puppies fell asleep to the thrum of the tires on the highway. Daniel held Tasha's hand the whole way, offering her comfort, even as he made several phone calls, arranging for his private plane to meet them, for a car and hotel in LA, and to let Matt know his plans.

Tasha's eyes widened as they pulled into Matt's

driveway, the gates standing open for them. It was like something out of a plantation in the Old South. Except that instead of a stable, there was a six-car garage.

The front door blew open before they'd had time to climb out of the truck. The whirlwind that flew down the front steps was Noah.

"Uncle Daniel!" Matt's son ran with his arms held wide, and Daniel scooped up the little boy, hugging him tight.

"Hey, bud. You're bigger every time I see you." He was six now and would be entering first grade in the fall.

Noah squirmed in his arms. "Can I see the puppies? Please, please, please, can I, can I?"

His smile spreading, Daniel opened the back door and let Noah climb inside. The child fell silent, in awe of the puppies that he would be taking care of for a few days.

Hand in hand, Matt and Ari followed Noah at a more sedate pace. "Thanks for helping out," Daniel said as he gave Ari a hug.

She was sweet and caring and absolutely right for Matt and Noah. Matt and his son were a package deal, and Ari had fallen hard for both of them. As hard as they'd fallen for her. Daniel couldn't say he'd ever seen a more loving mother, except his own.

As Tasha rounded the hood of his truck, he said, "Tasha, this is Ari."

She went to shake Ari's hand, but the other woman

hugged her instead. "It's so nice to meet you, Ari. Matt was so helpful at my cabin." She smiled shyly at him. "I really appreciate everything you did." Though she seemed a little nervous, she hugged him too.

"Believe me," Ari said, "he was delighted to dig into some hard physical labor. All the guys were." She turned, tucking Tasha's arm in hers. "I'm so sorry about your dad's illness. If you can spare five minutes, I'm putting together some things in the kitchen for you to take with you if you get hungry later. We all know how bad hospital food is."

After Tasha nodded and said that would be great, they headed inside, leaving Daniel and Matt with Noah and the puppies.

"Are you sure Ari's okay with taking care of three puppies?" Daniel asked.

"Are you kidding? She wanted to dash out here with Noah."

Going to retrieve the puppies, they found Noah seated on the floorboards, fingers clutched in the bars, his face plastered to the crate hard enough to put lines on his cheeks. Daniel unhooked the seat belt he'd laced through the bars of the crate to keep it stable, pulled it out, then carried it up the steps, Noah scurrying alongside.

"They're pretty much housebroken," he told Matt once they were inside the foyer, "as long as you let them sleep in their crate and remember to take them outside every couple of hours. But they make it through the whole night."

"Which one is mine, Uncle Daniel?" Noah asked. "Can I hold him?"

"It's this little guy here." He didn't give a name, because Noah would need to pick his own for the puppy.

Of course, once Daniel opened the crate, all three rushed out, running around maniacally after having been cooped up and sleeping for so long. Noah joined the melee, happily chasing them.

★ ★ ★

Tasha had felt lightheaded since Drew's call, her heart beating wildly with fear and dread. She couldn't believe her father might actually die. He'd always been larger than life. Impervious to the colds and broken bones that had felled lesser men.

The only thing that had gotten her through was Daniel's hand wrapped around hers as he drove. His warmth had flowed into her, calmed her, wore down the sharp edges of fear.

Now bright, sweet, kind Ari was taking over, pulling Tasha along into the kitchen where she was putting together the fixings for what looked like a feast to take on the plane.

"Here," Ari said, handing her a glass of Chardonnay. "I know it's the middle of the day, but sometimes gulping a glass of wine is exactly what we need to take the edge off."

Grateful beyond measure, Tasha did just as she suggested, and warmth immediately flowed through her veins. "You have a lovely home."

"The first time I walked in here," Ari said, "I thought it was a palace. I'm sure the guys told you I was Noah's nanny. I didn't come from much, so I assumed someone this rich was going to be stuck up and arrogant and bossy."

"But Matt isn't like that." Tasha knew firsthand. "None of the Mavericks are." They'd all been sweet to her. And so normal. Money had never gone to their heads; it was just another tool in their belts.

"Exactly." Ari beamed, her smile as bright as sunshine.

Her straight, silky blond hair didn't look salon dyed and styled, and her flowery sundress, though very pretty, wasn't haute couture. And her eyes shone with adoration whenever she said Noah's name. And Matt's.

The wine Tasha had gulped made her bold enough to say, "You're telling me I shouldn't be intimidated by Daniel's wealth and that he's just a normal guy, aren't you?"

"I don't know if *normal* is the word I would use," Ari said with a grin. "But definitely one of the nicest guys on the planet, that's for sure. I adore him." Her grin widened as she said, "Seems like you do too."

"I do." Tasha adored every part of him. But—"We haven't known each other that long."

"Sometimes it only takes one look," Ari said with

perfect certainty. With that, she put the last container into the insulated bag. "That should keep you from getting hungry for a good long while. And now I know you're anxious to get on your way."

The front hall was a madhouse, with three puppies and a little boy chasing each other. Daniel stood talking to a tall guy with short, dark-blond hair whom Tasha assumed was Gideon Smith, Ari's long-lost brother. On the drive down, Daniel had told her a bit about him, that he now worked for Daniel and lived with Ari and Matt. Gideon didn't smile much, not like his sister.

Noah ran to Ari as soon as he saw her, Spanky in his arms. "Can I have this one, Mommy? Daddy said I had to ask."

Ari flashed a smile at Matt. "Your daddy and I have talked about it, and yes, it's okay with me." She got down on his level. "But we've got to train him and take care of him and clean up after him too. That's a huge responsibility. Are you sure you want to do it?"

"Yes!"

Ari squeezed his hand. "Then let's take them all outside for a little bit so they don't make any messes in here."

Tasha's heart ached with the love she saw among the three of them, a family unit. It didn't matter that Ari had been the nanny, that she wasn't Noah's birth mother. They made a beautiful, loving family.

Tasha wanted to believe Daniel when he said it was time to forgive herself. That she could have a life again, a good one.

But could she really deserve all *this*? Not the money, but the happiness that was a shining halo around Ari. It was in the light of her eyes when she looked at Noah, the sweetness of her hand in Matt's.

Could Tasha ever truly deserve a man like Daniel and a family like the Mavericks?

Chapter Twenty-Five

The flight took barely an hour, and a car waited to drive them straight to the hospital. As they pulled beneath the hospital's portico, Tasha's heart began to jackhammer in her chest and her blood pounded in her ears.

Especially when they learned that her father hadn't been admitted under the name Summerfield.

The smells, antiseptic and sterile, turned her stomach. Soft-soled shoes screeched on the linoleum floors. The elevator walls closed in on her. The one positive thing she held on to was that Daniel had learned at Reception that her father wasn't in ICU or even CCU, the coronary care unit. Which meant he wasn't critical, thank God.

"Thank you," she said to Daniel as the elevator doors slid open silently. "I couldn't do this without you."

He'd done everything—helped find her family, flown her to the hospital, arranged a car. He'd even booked a hotel room for later, in case she was too tired to head back to San Francisco tonight.

But more than that, he'd simply *been* there, a solid warmth surrounding her, giving her comfort when she needed it most.

She'd lost her ability to trust when her father sold her out. But in this moment, she trusted Daniel with everything. And knew, deep within her heart, that he'd never betray her.

Ever.

Her father was in a private room. It made her sick to think he had paid for it with stolen money, but she still knocked on the door.

Drew opened it. "Thank God you're here, Tash."

In the three months since she'd seen him, her brother's short, dark hair had grown scraggly. His shirt was rumpled, his jeans baggy, his face gaunt, and his eyes sunken in dark circles. He looked ten years older.

She threw herself into his arms, hugging him so tightly her muscles hurt. Drew hugged her just as hard.

Then she stepped back to say, "This is Daniel Spencer." Daniel shook her brother's hand as though Drew were an equal, rather than a man who'd helped bilk people out of their money. "Daniel, this is my brother, Drew."

Drew's eyes widened, obviously realizing who Daniel was.

"Before we go in—" She pulled her brother into the hall. "What's going on?"

He closed the door. "Dad was complaining of chest pains and trouble breathing. We thought it was a heart attack, but—" He glanced back and lowered his voice as if their father could hear through the door. "His doctor was here just a few minutes ago and now they think he might have had a panic attack. The symptoms can sometimes mimic a heart attack."

Her father was the least panicky person she knew, always in control. But maybe that was just a lie too. Still, she was grateful to feel the weight of her fear that her father might die lift off her like a rising air balloon. Yet there was anger too, a simmering anger she felt guilty about when Drew needed her to be strong.

"They want to monitor him overnight," Drew went on. "I'm sorry I made you come all the way down here just for a panic attack. But I was worried." With a deep sigh that revealed his rattled emotions, he added, "And I wanted to see you."

She held his hand tightly. "Of course you had to call me. Daniel brought me as soon as humanly possible."

"I told Dad you were coming," Drew said. "He thought it was a bad idea."

"Why?" She snapped her teeth shut on the word. "Because he didn't want to worry me? Or because he thought I'd turn him in?"

"Tash." Her brother's dark eyes pleaded with her.

She felt Daniel at her side then, his strength seeping into her. She didn't want to turn into a bitter person because of her family.

She knew she had to forgive herself. But did the

path to that mean forgiving her father first?

She took a deep breath. "I better go in and see him."

The room was small, with a bathroom cubicle, a chair, a tray table, and enough room for the medical machines that monitored her father's vital signs.

She almost didn't recognize the man lying in the bed. Like Drew, his cheeks were gaunt. His steel-gray hair was dull, his skin sallow, his jowls hanging. The imposing figure was gone, and all that remained was a frail old man.

And it terrified her.

"Daddy." She hadn't called him that since she was a child, and maybe she did so now because she needed him to be the big, all-powerful father he'd once been.

Except that man had been an illusion.

Daniel's hand squeezed hers, and she drew courage from him. He possessed true strength made up of kindness and heart.

With Daniel by her side, she was able to take her father's hand. "How are you feeling?"

"I'm fine," he tried to bluster, but he no longer had the power for that. "I don't need to be here. Drew's just an old biddy."

"You might have been having a heart attack. He did the right thing."

"Bah," her father grumbled. "And who's he?" He jutted his chin at Daniel.

"This is Daniel. He brought me here to see you."

And I love him.

Drew broke in before their father could make a derogatory comment. "Thank you for bringing Tasha. We appreciate it."

Daniel tipped his head slightly in acknowledgment. "She needed to be here." He squeezed her hand. "And I needed to be here for her."

His words and his solid presence warmed her. There was so much in that simple statement.

Her brother's gaze flashed from Daniel and back to her, and she knew Drew could see the importance of their relationship. So did her father, his brow furrowing.

"Dad." She wouldn't call him Daddy again. The past was gone, and the man she'd thought he was had never truly existed. "We need to talk." She let go of Daniel's hand to take her father's in both of hers. "About what happened. About the resort."

Her father sank back against the pillow. "I'm tired."

"It was a panic attack." She wouldn't have pushed if he'd had a heart attack. But with nurses and doctors just outside the door to tend to him, she decided he was well enough to answer her questions.

"I'm still tired."

"And we still need to talk. I've had a lot of time to think." She tightened her hold on his hand when he closed his eyes. "In fact, I've been angry with myself for not seeing the truth."

His hand was weak in hers, not returning her grip,

and for a long moment, she thought he would ignore her. But at last he opened his eyes. "You weren't supposed to see. I wanted to shield you. That's why I made you an outside contractor, so you wouldn't be affected by any of it."

"For God's sake," Drew burst out, "tell her the truth, Dad. She deserves it after everything we've put her through. And I deserve it too."

Her father pierced him with a long look, but her brother didn't back down. Tension simmered in the air between them like steam rising.

"All right, if you really want to know the truth, your brother is the one who insisted on making you a subcontractor. And he insisted on not letting you go to the site. But I concurred that it was better to keep you at arm's length."

Drew stood then, his back suddenly straight and some of the haggard strain leaving his face. "You're not tainted by this, Tasha. No one ever blamed you or thought any of this was your fault."

Daniel tensed. She sensed his need to do battle for her, but she couldn't let him. Three months ago, instead of fighting, she'd run to the mountains, licking her wounds. But she was stronger than that. She knew it now, even if she hadn't known it before.

With a hand on Daniel's arm, she willed him to relax. Then she said what had to be said. "You're wrong, Drew. I am tainted, by all the lies if nothing else. But I love you for trying to make me believe I'm not."

Her family wasn't Daniel's family. They weren't good or pure. But they were *her* family, and no matter what, she could never stop loving them, flaws and all. She didn't have to be like them, but she wouldn't stop loving them.

She'd blamed herself, her blindness, but it was time to forgive. Daniel had taught her that, but she hadn't believed, not until this moment, when she saw how the seeds of her blindness had been born.

Out of love.

"I understand now." She gazed at her father for long, agonizing moments, at his haggard features, his downhill slide. "I love you, Dad. I always have and I always will, no matter what you've done. Because you made me feel loved. But I'm not a child anymore, and I can't stand by and watch you destroy Drew. And I won't watch you destroy other people either. You have to stop making excuses, saying that it was okay because I was only a subcontractor."

"But it was only greedy people looking to get rich quick," her father insisted.

She held up a hand to stop him from saying more. For the first time, her father shushed. She sensed Daniel's outrage in his bristling body, and her outrage equaled his.

"Don't you *dare* try to justify what you do," she said. "You're not Robin Hood. You're not some sort of do-gooder." She narrowed her eyes to a glare. "And if your lies and cheating and stealing weren't bad enough, you dragged Drew into it."

"Your brother—" her father started.

She couldn't bear another excuse, so she turned to Drew. "Tell me the truth. Do you really want this for the rest of your life? To go on stealing? Because that's what it is."

"I'm tired." His cracked voice sounded so weary. "And I'm done. I've been done since…" He shook his head sadly. "Since I lost you three months ago, Tash."

He'd lost her the first time he'd helped her father with one of his schemes. Because he'd lost himself. But now that they'd found each other again, she wanted so badly to believe him. And to believe *in* him.

Maybe this was one of those times when looking on the bright side and seeing the best in people wasn't a flaw.

She might end up being wrong for giving her brother a second chance. But she sensed that her belief in him would help the brother she loved actually become the good person he was capable of being. If she had faith in Drew and was there to buoy him up if he ever doubted, then maybe he could eventually find the will to trust in himself.

Maybe that's what family was all about. Believing in them enough to make sure they believed in themselves. Just as Daniel's mother believed in every one of her kids.

She went to her brother and took his hands in hers.

"I believe in you, Drew."

"You shouldn't."

But she wasn't that easily scared away. Not anymore. "I *do*."

Then she turned back to her father. "Before I leave tonight, you're going to promise me two things."

"What?" Her father looked mulish. But also a little cowed by her.

"That you're going to pay back *every single penny* to *every single person* you owe."

"Impossible!"

"I'm sure you have records of all of them," she replied in a firm tone. "And if not, I'm happy to find them for you and send each one a personal note to let them know their money is on its way back to them. Got it?"

He looked like a chastised child, pouting after being caught with his hand in the cookie jar. "Fine."

"Good. And second, you're going to stop your cons, once and for all. If I find out that you haven't—and believe me, I will—I'll make sure the feds have enough information about what you've done to lock you up. Forever."

He stared at her. For a long while. "You've changed."

"I have." She wouldn't apologize for finally finding her strength. "And now it's time for you to change. Long past time."

His mouth was set in a firm line. But he nodded.

Tasha felt as though she'd sprinted an entire marathon. But she still had one more very important thing to say. "I love you both. You're my family. I only want you to be able to do what's good and what's right. That's all I've ever wanted."

Her father picked at the white sheets. No matter what he said, she believed the things he'd done weighed on him. The panic attack proved it.

Or, if she took off her rose-colored glasses, maybe he was just afraid of getting caught.

But even if her father was a lost cause, she believed in Drew. Her brother could change—and she wouldn't give up on him until he did.

Gathering Daniel's hand in hers, leaning into him for the comfort he had always been so quick to give, she said to her brother, "Tell me where you've been the past three months."

And she listened to their story.

★ ★ ★

Daniel was so damn proud of Tasha, his heart felt near to bursting. Even as he'd wanted to crush her old man for what he'd done to her, for the pain he'd caused, for his betrayal. For making Tasha lose her ability to trust. For making her doubt herself.

Daniel wanted to help her heal, and healing was in every word she'd said. She'd gone to bat for her brother and hadn't accepted her father's excuses. But neither had she withheld her love.

Love was the most important thing.

No matter what her family had done.

It was something he wished his mother and father had realized about themselves long before now. His mother had forgiven everyone else—but she hadn't forgiven herself. If she had, she never would have kept her secrets from him. She would never have been afraid of what he'd think of her.

He could only hope that after their conversation, she'd finally seen that she had nothing to ask his forgiveness for. In fact, his mother had helped him find Tasha, to accept Tasha just the way she was.

No one was perfect. But Tasha was still perfect for him.

It was after midnight by the time they left her father's room. It had been a long, long day, and she leaned into him as they rode the elevator to the penthouse suite he'd booked. He'd wanted to give her luxury, something she could totally unwind in, with a jetted tub, thick comforters, and the softest mattress.

Inside the suite, he sat her down on the sofa in the sunken living room and went to one knee in front of her to remove her sandals.

A colossal fruit basket sat on the coffee table, compliments of Walter Braedon, owner of the Regent Hotel. In addition, champagne chilled in a bucket, and two crystal flutes sparkled in the lamplight.

She flopped back against the sofa, and when he began to massage her feet, she groaned her appreciation.

Her eyes closed, she asked, "Do you think my father will change?"

"I don't know." He always wanted to be honest with her. "But your brother already has."

They'd left him in her father's sick room. The two had roamed the country for the last three months, never staying any one place for long, always paying cash, which meant they'd slept in cheap motels that didn't require credit cards, eaten fast food, and probably drunk too much as well.

"Do you know what I think? Your brother only stayed because he thought your father needed him." Daniel worked up her right leg, then the other, unknotting her calf muscles.

"That feels so good." Opening her eyes, she held out her hand. "But come here beside me. I want to apologize."

He gathered her into his arms, the place he always wanted her to be. "You have nothing to apologize for."

"I do. When we first met, I was mean to you."

He laughed. "You really don't know the meaning of *mean*." He'd loved her feistiness, her banter.

"I refused everything, questioned everything, like your intentions were suspect. Like you weren't worth trusting."

"Sweetheart," he whispered. "What else were you going to think about some strange guy after what you'd been through with your own family?"

She shook her head. "The thing is, I did my friends

a disservice too. I left them in order to punish myself. But I ended up punishing them as well. I want them back. I want to explain everything and make it right again."

He laid his hand over hers. "They'll understand."

"I hope so. It's taken me a while, but I think I finally see what your story about Whitney and your mom and Evan really means." She looked into his eyes. "If you never believe in people, if you can't see the good in them, then you can never truly believe in yourself. So if I want Drew to see the good in himself, I *have* to see it too. And if I want my friends back, I have to believe we can all forgive." She gave him a small smile, but one that lit her eyes. "Even ourselves."

His heart swelled, and the words came out of him in a rush.

"That's exactly what I want my mother to hear. That she needs to forgive herself. It's as important as forgiving other people. Maybe more so."

"What could your mother possibly have done that needs forgiveness? She's perfect."

"My mother is incredible. But no one is perfect." When Tasha's eyebrows went up in question, he explained, "I'd been getting these weird signals from her ever since I came to the mountains. Like there was something she was hiding from me, something that made her really uncomfortable. She even hung up on me once."

"Why?"

"It turns out that she got pregnant with me before she and my dad were married. And she ran away from him. She didn't even tell him about me."

Tasha looked shocked. "What was she planning to do?"

"Her mom wanted her to give me away, but she insisted on keeping me. She just wasn't going to tell Dad." Then he told Tasha the whole story.

Talking about it wasn't a betrayal of his mom, it was an affirmation of everything she'd been through.

And it was an affirmation of everything Tasha had gone through as well.

"I always thought the perfect relationship meant that you never argued, you never hit any bumps in the road, you always saw eye to eye on everything, that you never kept a secret or made a mistake that hurt the one you loved." He cupped Tasha's cheek, stroked his finger over her bottom lip. "But now I can see that *perfect* simply means learning how to forgive and to accept and to do everything you can to love with your whole heart."

She turned into his touch, kissing his palm. "I was afraid I might not be worthy of your family. That they were pillars of strength I could never live up to. But it turns out that they're human, just like me."

"Like me too." He let his gaze wander over every strong, striking feature of her face. "It was your love that helped me realize I had to be brave enough to talk to my mom. To ask her what was wrong."

"I love that we've given each other strength," she said. "Your love helped me face my father and my love helped you talk with your mom. You and me together—we feel exactly right. Maybe," she said with a grin, "even a little bit perfect."

Chapter Twenty-Six

Tasha didn't know how long they held each other. All she knew was that she'd never been so happy, never felt so good. So whole. "I want to make love with you, Daniel. I want to give you everything the way you've always given everything to me."

"You've already done that."

He lifted her, and she wrapped her legs around his waist as he carried her to the dark bedroom. Her feet slid to the carpet, but she stayed on tiptoe, her head tipped back so she could see his beautiful, amazing face. Giving him *everything* started with confessing the last of her fears.

"When I saw your apartment today—and your plane—and Matt's house—I was afraid. Of how rich you are. Of how hard it could be to live up to all that."

"You know my money doesn't mean anything."

"But it does. It's what all my father's dirty deeds were about. Money is…" She searched for the right words, desperately needing him to understand. "Money is something you earn. It's not something you deserve. And for a while today, I started to lose ground, because I was afraid I didn't deserve you. That I hadn't been good enough. That I'd made too many mistakes, and I hadn't paid enough for them. And yes, I didn't believe that I deserved your family either. But with my father tonight, I realized what I needed to deserve wasn't your money, but your strength. Your loyalty. Your love." She held his face in her hands just as he had held hers. "I'm making a promise to you, right here, right now, that I will never stop giving all those things to you, just the way you've always given them to me."

He crushed her to him then, and together they fell to the bed.

"You're everything to me," he vowed. "I never dreamed you would fall into my life."

"From a roof, no less," she said with a smile that was full of more joy than she'd ever known was possible.

★ ★ ★

"I love you," he whispered against her lips before he parted them and went deep. Tasted her, tasted sweetness, tasted love. "You are so beautiful, inside and out." He would never cease to be amazed by her. "I'm going to make love to you for the rest of my life." It was a promise, a vow.

He reached between them, pulling her clothes off, his fingers grazing her until she shivered with the erotic contact. Reveling in the heat of her, in the bounty of her breasts, he lavished kisses on the pearled tips. Then finally she was naked. He tore at his clothes, because the only thing in the world he needed now was her skin against his.

He entered her with a slow reverence, their bodies generating heat like the inside of a volcano.

"*Daniel.*" She arched, pushed her head back into the mattress, taking him deeper ever so slowly.

The times they'd had each other were out of this world, but after everything they'd revealed to each other, this was a true communion. He needed to relish each moment of it. Every moment of *her*.

He went to his knees, holding himself inside her, draping her legs over his thighs. "Tasha," he whispered. "I'll remember the sight of you like this forever."

Her skin was tinged pink, her eyes half-lidded with desire, her lips moist and red from his kisses. He ran his fingers over her stomach, savoring her, then finally dropped to her hips and pulled her tight against him.

She rewarded him with a delicious moan. "Please," she begged.

He held her, moved slowly inside her, so damn slowly it was exquisite torture. "Do you feel that?"

She cried out, her hands on his arms, her body clutching him from the inside, and he breathed harshly to stave off his own pleasure. As she dug her heels into the mattress, all her muscles tightening, he found her perfect spot and rode it relentlessly, his strokes short and slow. Driving them both to the edge of wildness.

It was all he could do not to lose control as her body tightened and released, squeezed and rolled. She moved with him, unconsciously trying to take him deeper, harder, faster.

His blood pounded, his body wanting to unleash, yet his mind needed this. Flushed with arousal, her lips parted, her breasts rising, falling, every muscle tensed. And the glorious sight of him filling her, the intimate connection, the ultimate ownership, his and hers.

Then he moved his hands between her thighs and Tasha went wild, crying out her pleasure, grabbing his arms, her nails biting where she held him, her body spasming around him.

Until the moment he couldn't hold out a second longer, falling on her, thrusting high and deep, her cries filling him up. There was only her, the pleasure, the feel of her around him, and the explosion rocketing through him as she dragged him into the glorious wildness with her.

* * *

Tasha woke in the morning to the scent of coffee and bacon and toast, and the sound of the suite's front door closing. Daniel had slung a fluffy robe across the foot of the bed for her, and she drew its thick folds around her, feeling lusciously naked beneath the soft material.

Delicious scents drew her out to the living room. Daniel wore the matching robe, the lapels hanging open to reveal tanned skin that she wanted to kiss all over, just the way she had last night.

"Coffee?" He held up the pot. "Or juice."

Wrapping her arms around him from behind, she whispered in his ear, *"You."*

He pulled her around to sit in his lap, kissing her breathless. "If you keep doing that," he told her, "our breakfast will get cold."

"I don't mind if breakfast gets cold."

Of course, that was right when Daniel's phone rang again. Somehow, she guessed it was her brother, even before Daniel said the words.

She already knew why Drew was calling, had known it every moment that she was with her father in the hospital room. All the belief in the world couldn't change someone who didn't want to change. At least, not this quickly.

She climbed off Daniel to take the phone from him, but he pulled her to his lap again, giving her his strength. Just as they'd promised each other, he would always be there whenever she needed him.

With his arms around her, she said, "Hello."

"Dad is gone," Drew said bluntly. "I went out for coffee, and he was gone when I got back."

"I knew he would go." She didn't sugarcoat it. "And I'm glad he didn't try to pull you back in when he left."

"I wouldn't have run with him, Tash. I'm turning myself in. I'm sick to death of running. I'll take what-ever they throw at me. I meant it when I said I was done. No more lies. Ever."

She leaned into Daniel's shoulder, feeling sick at the thought of what would happen to Drew. But also knowing he needed to face the consequences. "I'm proud of you for owning up to everything. I'm here in any way you need me."

"I love you, Tash. And I'm sorry. So damned sorry, I wish I could rewind back to eighteen and make very different choices."

"Those choices made us who we are," she said softly. Amazingly, they'd brought her to Daniel. "I'll help any way I can, just please call to let me know what's going to happen to you once you talk to the authorities."

They said their good-byes, then Daniel held her tightly. "I take it your father is in the wind?"

"Yes."

His muscles tensed. "Do you want me to find him? I can. I will."

"No. Just like Drew, he has to make that decision himself, whether he wants to pay for what he did or run for the rest of his life. And maybe for now, that's what he thinks he still wants." She sighed. "It might be crazy for me to believe this, but I have to keep the faith that losing his family will force him to change."

For long, beautiful, agonizing moments, Daniel simply held her, his lips against her hair. Then he said, "I can get a good lawyer for Drew. I'll pay for him too."

His sweetness and caring brought tears to her eyes. "Thank you. But I can't let you pay for anything."

"We're partners. And now your brother is my family too. He's doing the right thing, and I want to help him."

"Thank you," she whispered again, choking back the sob that rose up.

"One more thing," he murmured against her hair.

"Anything."

"Anything?" He had a wicked glint in his eyes, one that boded *very* well for her.

"Yes, anything."

"Okay then." He slid her from his arms, settling her back on the chair as he went down on one knee. "Marry me."

She threw her arms around him, her love for him so great she didn't think her body could contain it. "*Yes.*"

Epilogue

The Fourth of July was blazingly hot out by Matt's pool. The kids, and most of the adults too, were staying cool in the water.

Daniel was glad to find a rare moment alone with his mother while Tasha was playing with kids and puppies. Both Jeremy and Noah were ecstatic that their little furry friends would finally be able to stay with them.

"They are absolutely adorable," Mom said.

"Yes, they all are."

Especially his gorgeous, talented, smart, and sexy Tasha. He'd never been happier. He'd always known love would do that; he just hadn't realized how many different meanings there could be for the word *perfect*. And Tasha was finally happy too.

She'd connected with her friends and reestablished her business. The clients were rolling in again. She was crafting some super-secret special interactive program that would be an adjunct to his how-to videos. That was all he knew, since she shut down her computer every time he entered the room so her huge surprise wouldn't be spoiled. Whatever it was would be magnificent, he was certain of it.

Her gray clouds were gone, her shadows dispelled. She was the woman who had been lurking beneath the surface that first day he followed her into her cabin.

And he never wanted to leave.

Daniel slipped his hand around his mom's, squeezing. "I have you to thank for finding Tasha."

She smiled softly, watching the puppies and kids wrestling and rolling on the grass. "I wish I could say that were true. But you found her all on your own. I wasn't much help this time. More of a hindrance, I'd say."

A weight seemed to have been lifted with the confession she'd made over a month ago during that long phone call. Yet he feared his mother was still walking under her own cloud.

Raising their clasped hands, he kissed her knuckles. "That's what I really wanted to talk to you about. You seem to be under the mistaken impression that it was a bad thing to allow me to grow up thinking all marriages had to be perfect."

"It made your expectations far too high."

"Do you remember what you said the day you told me I was a twinkle in your eye before you and Dad got married?"

She pursed her lips, but he sensed the smile there. "What a lovely way of describing my indiscretion. But I said a lot of things during that phone call."

"Ah, but the most important thing you said was that you loved me just the way I am. That if you hadn't gotten pregnant with me exactly when you did, I would have been someone completely different."

"You're right. You wouldn't have been my Daniel." She cupped his cheek, moisture glistening in her eyes. "And I would have missed you so much."

"Don't you see that's exactly the way I feel about Tasha? If my expectations about the perfect marriage, the perfect relationship, and the perfect wife had been any different, I might have missed finding her. I might have taken another path that didn't lead me to her. So what you taught me, Mom, is that everything happens exactly the way it's supposed to."

"Oh sweetheart." She leaned her head on his shoulder as Tasha saw them and waved. "I'm so glad you finally know everything. And that you've found the love you deserve."

"Tasha completes me, Mom."

"I know exactly what you mean."

"Because it's the way Dad completes you?"

"Yes. And Will and Harper, Sebastian and Charlie, Matt and Ari, Evan and Paige. I'm so happy for every single one of my boys."

"I love you, Mom. I always have and I always will. You never did anything wrong. You never needed to feel guilty, so I want you to promise me that you will forgive yourself for whatever mistakes you think you made. And I don't want you to ever feel like you need to hide anything from me either. Because I will never judge you. In fact, knowing what you and Dad went through, I admire both of you even more. If anything, I feel more loved because of what you sacrificed to keep me with you."

"Oh honey, thank you. I love you so much." She sniffed, then she looked past him to her big brood of Mavericks. "I love all of you. Every single one of my boys and the wonderful families you're building."

He kissed the top of her head. Then he smiled across the lawn at the woman snuffling her face into the fluffy, furry belly of a squirming puppy. The beautiful, perfect woman with whom he would spend the rest of his life.

* ★ ★

Sitting under the canopy covering several lounge chairs, Gideon Jones nursed a beer, watching.

They were a cheerful bunch, these Mavericks. He was happy that Ari had found Matt and Noah. Matt was a good man, worthy of her, and she was as radiant as the child she'd been when Gideon had left her behind to join the Army.

The two would be married by the end of the summer, and she would truly become Noah's mother. Her love for the kid shone right out of her, like a beacon for all the world to see.

She'd grown into a beautiful woman, and he was so damn proud of her. But it was something he could never seem to find the words to tell her. He'd lost the ability to express the things he felt. He'd seen too much during his eight years in the service.

But he didn't think about those lost years. He didn't think about the past.

He simply watched other people living their lives. Sometimes he even smiled. Like now.

Sebastian Montgomery had actually talked Francine Ballard into the water. Charlie's mother was a dear old soul, crippled with arthritis, but always with a kind word, even for him.

"Oh my goodness," she trilled as Sebastian carried her down into the water. She wore a flowered bathing suit with a high neck and a skirt that covered her thighs.

"The water will be good for you, Mom. We should have thought of this years ago." Charlie held her hands and danced her along the edge of the shallow end while Sebastian hovered close by in case he was needed.

"She's a darling, isn't she?" Susan Spencer had come to sit beside Gideon. In her mid-fifties, with a cap of gray hair, she was vital and dynamic, moving so softly he hadn't heard her. Daniel had flown his parents and sister in from Chicago for the July Fourth celebration.

"Yes, she is," Gideon agreed.

"Why aren't you in there, honey, playing Marco Polo?"

"I'm feeling lazy today."

But the truth was that he didn't feel like one of them. He was still an outsider despite the eight months that had passed since he'd walked back into his sister's life.

He felt the ache and anger and hopelessness that had been his constant companions for years now. He'd been in the Middle East when his mom died. He'd lost track of Ari. She'd ended up in foster care. He hadn't saved her.

Having exhausted the trio of puppies—who were now lolling in the shade until they got their second wind—the kids were splashing in the pool, yelling "Marco!" and "Polo!" and having great fun with Matt and the other Mavericks. Jeremy and Will played too, plus Ari, Chi, and Rosie and Jorge. Chi and Rosie, Ari's best friends, the girls she'd survived foster care with, were part of the family now. Along with Jorge, Rosie's son. He and Noah had become best friends too.

The Maverick ladies, including Daniel's sister, Lyssa, were sunning themselves, a bevy of beauties in bright colors.

Bob Spencer, the patriarch of the clan, manned the barbecue. A charcoal smell wafted on the air.

"Bob, honey," Susan called. "You're not burning the burgers, are you?"

"No, dear, I'd never do that," he singsonged back.

A more loving couple he'd never seen—expect for the Mavericks and their ladies. Even when they were nattering, they were good-natured about it.

"Daniel," Susan hissed loudly. "Your father needs some help."

Daniel Spencer climbed out of the pool where he'd been canoodling with Tasha Summerfield in the deep end, where the children didn't venture. Tasha followed him, wearing a ball cap that read *Everything's better with my tool belt on.*

Daniel had always seemed a happy guy, laid-back in his work approach, at least for the most part. But with Tasha, he was somehow more than just *happy.* Gideon wasn't sure how to describe it to himself. Ari said it was love. And she should know.

Tasha Summerfield was a different genus from the rest of them. Her father was a con man, and her brother was doing community service for his part in their father's schemes. Daniel had probably paid the lawyers *beaucoup* bucks to get the guy a sweet deal in which he did his service at a foundation—set up by Daniel—to help the victims of fraud. And to teach people how to spot a con and run in the opposite direction.

"How's everything going with the job?" Susan asked. "You've been such a great help to Daniel."

She wasn't a busybody, or prying. He understood that. She simply cared. And she loved her kids.

"It's good," he said.

He'd worked for Daniel for close to eight months now. He'd thought he'd be spending his time in the stores, but Daniel had been giving him more managerial responsibilities, dealing with suppliers and materials.

He was even trying to talk Gideon into coming on his DIY show.

"You're a man of few words," Susan said mildly. "I like that about you."

That forced a laugh out of Gideon.

The French doors opened, and the last arrivals spilled onto the deck. Susan jumped up to greet Evan, his arm slung around Paige. Evan's birth mom—versus Susan, who was more like his real mom—and the twins had come too. Tony and Kelsey, the twin brother and sister Evan hadn't known about until a few months ago. At twenty-five, Tony was the image of Evan, but Kelsey was the prettier of the two.

The Maverick family had become a clan over the last few months. Gideon was probably considered one of them, especially since he was living with Ari and Matt. But he needed to get out soon, before they became newlyweds. They would need their space, despite the fact that the house was a mansion with eight bedrooms and a bowling alley and home theater in the basement.

No, he had to go.

The kids climbed out of the pool and dashed to the newcomers, with Rosie and Ari calling, "Don't run," after them, as they too got out of the pool, streaming water.

Noah grabbed Tony's hand, then Kelsey's, pulling

them. "You gotta come and see the puppies. There's one for me and one for Jeremy and one for Uncle Daniel."

Gideon stood, setting his beer on the side table to say hello. Once that was done, he could take to the background where he preferred to be.

Ari passed him, bussing his cheek with a quick kiss. "You need to get in the water, big brother. Have some fun with us."

But he'd long ago forgotten how to have fun.

Then Jorge grabbed his hand, looking up at him with imploring dark-chocolate eyes just like Rosie's. He was a great kid. "Come on, Gid, you gotta play Marco Polo with us."

His heart seemed to rise up in his throat as he remembered the games he and Ari used to play. It didn't matter that he was ten years older, he'd always found the time for whatever game she loved.

But that was long ago. And he'd been another person.

Rosie grabbed his other hand. "Or we're going to throw you in." She grinned at him.

Together, she and Jorge pulled him along with the force of their laughter.

"Come on," the others called. Maverick voices, Jeremy, Ari, and Chi. Even Francine.

Then the guys tackled him and tossed him in.

He had no choice but to become a part of them.

At least for now.

ABOUT THE AUTHORS

Having sold more than 7 million books, *New York Times* and *USA Today* bestselling author Bella Andre's novels have been #1 bestsellers around the world. Known for "sensual, empowered stories enveloped in heady romance" (*Publishers Weekly*), her books have been *Cosmopolitan* magazine "Red Hot Reads" twice and have been translated into ten languages. Winner of the Award of Excellence, *The Washington Post* has called her "One of the top digital writers in America" and she has been featured by *Entertainment Weekly*, NPR, *USA Today*, *Forbes*, *The Wall Street Journal* and, most recently, in *Time* magazine. She has given keynote speeches at publishing conferences from Copenhagen to Berlin to San Francisco, including a standing-room-only keynote at Book Expo America, on her publishing success.

New York Times and *USA Today* bestselling author Jennifer Skully is a lover of contemporary romance, bringing you poignant tales peopled with hilarious characters that will make you laugh and make you cry. Writing as Jasmine Haynes, she's authored over 35 classy, sensual romance tales about real issues like growing older, facing divorce, starting over. Her books have passion and heart and humor and happy endings, even if they aren't always traditional. She also writes gritty, paranormal mysteries in the Max Starr series. Having penned stories since the moment she learned to write, she now lives in the Redwoods of Northern California with her husband and their adorable nuisance of a cat who totally runs the household.

Newsletter signup:
http://bit.ly/SkullyNews

Jennifer's Website:
www.jenniferskully.com

Blog:
www.jasminehaynes.blogspot.com

Facebook:
facebook.com/jasminehaynesauthor

Twitter:
twitter.com/jasminehaynes1